AF480642

Vampire Legacy

By Bethlyn Hernandez
Cover art by Addyson Macona

This book is for each of you, my readers. It may be my first book, but it is also our first journey together. I truly hope it's a journey you will cherish as much as I have. A special thank you to my parents for always believing in my creativity, and making sure I know that if I really want to do something, I can. And especially to my old Teddy Bear, without whom this story never would have never had its beginning.

Prologue

It was the dead of night when Kel was awoken by her mother's scream. She walked to her parents' room, her favorite teddy bear dragging at her feet. The only light in the hallway came from the bright, full moon outside.

"Mommy…? Daddy…?" The five year old girl slowly pushed open the door to the master bedroom, lit only by the moonlight. She saw her father sprawled on the floor and a look of defiance in her mother's eyes.

"Kel… run…" The whisper was barely audible from the woman's lips as her eyes went blank, but Kel understood. Her parents had told her there were bad people in the world, and if the bad people ever came, she was supposed to hide in the little hideaway closet inside her bedroom closet. Kel knew what she had to do – but she was only five, her father was dead, she was frozen in fear as she watched her mother slowly fall to the floor, and the closet always had a weird garlicky sort of smell to it. Her mother had thought it was silly, but her father had insisted on garlic being in there.

The vampire that had taken her mother's life turned towards the little girl. Kel's eyes widened as he walked slowly towards her, with a look of derangement in his eyes. She took a faltering step backward and dropped her teddy bear. The way he looked at her was terrifying, and something clicked. If she didn't run now, there would be no second chance.

"No! Mommy! Daddy!" Kel screamed. As she turned to run, she tripped over her teddy bear and was caught in a pair of strong arms that easily held her in place, despite her thrashing. She cried, knowing her parents were gone forever, and that she would soon be gone, too. But as she felt the vampire's teeth come closer and closer to her neck, she felt warm. Almost as if her body knew she wasn't in any danger. Instead of the sharp fangs she expected, soft lips kissed her on the forehead. She looked up, astonished as the vampire took her back to her room and tucked her in.

"Sleep, little one. Luck seems to favor you tonight."

With trembling lips, the girl whispered "Why?" She couldn't understand it – how could he be so cruel to kill her parents and let her live? She felt sleep taking over her, but she still had to know.

A smile crept to his lips. "Maybe you will know one day. Until then, I must leave you." He handed her back her teddy bear.

She knew, even as young as she was, what she would have to do if she really lived through the night. "Name. What's your name?"

He gazed down at the little girl for a moment, as if considering whether or not to tell her, before answering. "Count Vito. I will watch over you, child, do not fear. Now sleep."

Determination showed in the girl's sleepy eyes as she nodded. She wouldn't be afraid. She would grow up strong and kill the vampire who stood in front of her now. It was her final thought before the overwhelming urge to sleep took over her small body.

Chapter 1

I heard a knock on my door and inwardly groaned. Twelve years have passed since I made the vow to myself to avenge my parents. I'll never forget his face or his name. How could I, when I've seen him lurking in the distance so many times over the years? Piercing blue eyes framed by light brown hair that seemed to always be combed back perfectly, Count Vito was the vampire who took everything from me except for my life. How could anyone have been so cruel? It would have been so much easier if he had taken my life that night, too. It would have saved me years of pain and longing. Those were years I could never get back – as the other children my age played without a care, I sat and plotted ways to become a vampire hunter and exact my revenge. I would find trees to practice fighting against, instead of playing games on the playground. Or I would borrow books from the nearby hunter academy to read in my spare time. I made myself an outcast – the adults had said I was aged beyond my years, but it paid off in the end. I looked up as my door slowly opened.

"Hey, you awake?" A head of short brown hair peeked into my door. It's Dustin. Again. He's been a royal pain since I got hurt and put practically on bed rest. I guess it's nice of him though, making sure I'm ok. But I can't fool myself into thinking it's more than just a partnership – we're linked through a common goal: hunting vampires. He'll hunt any of them, though he seems more serious when hunting Count Vito. I'll hunt them all, too, but my goal isn't really to rid the world of all vampires – just the one that killed my parents. And if I can't kill him, I hope he kills me.

"Yeah, I'm awake." I mumbled. I was still mad at myself for being too focused on Count Vito that night. *Stupid vampires always get in the way, now I have to be taken care of by my partner. I must look so weak. I hate looking weak.* Dustin walked into my room and smiled at me. Great, is he going to make fun of me now? A moment of silence passed before I couldn't stand it any longer. "So? What is it?"

"I just got back from buying some supplies and decided to check in on you for the millionth time."

"Million and one now." I rolled my eyes at him. At least being laid up didn't take my sarcasm from me. "I'm fine, I'm getting better, and I'll be up and about in just a couple more days." Dustin pulled a chair up next to my bed. I never did understand his motives, but ever since we decided to use my house as base, he's always been super protective of me. Like an older brother. But I don't want an older brother. I can't ever allow myself to get attached to someone again, in case I lose them. I sighed to myself softly as these thoughts went through my head. Dustin must've thought I was sighing at him. The look in his hazel eyes clouded over.

"Ok, well I'm sorry for disturbing you. I'll be in the kitchen putting a few things away, then I'm heading down to the basement to work out."

"Ok," I chewed my lip for a moment as my thoughts kept racing. "Hey, before you go – what's for lunch? Not soup again, is it?" I'm starting to think that's all he remembers how to make these days.

"That depends. What would you like?"

"What are you willing to make?" I fired off the question so quick, I hardly realized that I was saying it. I was suddenly ravenous.

"Anything the doctor was willing to let you eat. Good food for strength. You're going to need your strength for healing."

"You don't think I was actually paying attention to the doctor, do you? I never listen to doctors…" Who knew a doctor would be so strict about what I could eat when I had bruised ribs and a sprained ankle anyways? So what if it hurt to take a deep breath, why should that affect what I eat? And I've sprained my ankle a few times before in fights. I vaguely remember him saying I needed to eat certain foods to heal faster, but that was about it. Doctors who focused on vampire hunters were always overly strict. I crossed my arms and laid back on the pillow in annoyance as Dustin chuckled. I gazed out my bedroom window.

It was actually a beautiful day outside. A few puffy clouds dotted the blue sky, with the green, tree covered mountains making a picturesque backdrop. It was actually kind of nice to live in a town nestled between mountains. Most people who knew nothing about the existence of vampires tended to avoid our little towns, which made it easier for hunters to gather and talk freely.

Of course, the downside was that the mountains were covered in trees, which made navigating them during our searches for vampires a little more difficult, especially when the vamps knew we were coming and hid in trees to ambush us.

"I know, however I was."

"So I'm stuck on some stupid diet still, huh?"

"Kinda. It's hard being the world's youngest Vampire Hunter Academy graduate and being on bed rest, huh?" I was only 15 when I graduated. At my glare, he quickly changed his teasing tone to a helpful one. "Ramen noodles sound ok?"

"Fried chicken wasn't on the list, was it?"

"I don't think so. You know they want us to eat healthy, although ramen isn't really healthy, either. Besides, we don't have a deep fryer."

"Fine. Chicken ramen's ok."

"Ok. I'll be back in a few." I didn't even watch as he walked out. I mumbled my appreciation and turned the TV on to mindlessly watch the commercials. I never could move into my parents' room, and Dustin moved into the spare bedroom we had. It was supposed to be for the baby brother or sister I was going to have one day. Stupid vampire took my parents and sibling-to-be. All the things I would love to do to that creep... I didn't realize how long I was lost in thought until Dustin came back into my room with a food tray.

"Alright, we got chicken ramen noodles, a can of mountain dew, and, oh, look at that – I found a piece of chocolate cake for ya, too. And of course, a side of pain killers."

"Alright! You know what hits the spot Dustin! Heh, maybe I should stay wounded – I get someone to wait on me hand and foot." I smirked at him. We both knew I could never stay off my feet this long ever again.

Dustin looked smug. "Don't count on it girl. I'm just doing this until you feel up to doing it for yourself."

"Oh well," I scoffed. "It wasn't such a hot idea anyways. Too many guys would be competing to serve me, for my affections." I looked toward the wall with a lofty expression on my face.

"Ha! Get your head out of the clouds. Who would ever fight over you?" Ouch. I quickly turned my head toward him with a scowl on my face. So what if his voice was heavy with sarcasm? A girl can only take so many blows to her ego, and being injured counted as a lot of hits.

"Oh, 'ha' yourself! Lots of guys would fight over me, for your information!" I looked away from him, towards my light blue walls. As a child, I had expressed interest in the skies – I always wanted to learn about the stars and moon, sun and clouds. My parents were in the process of painting my room to look like a beautiful partly cloudy day outside before they were killed. I saw Dustin shaking his head out of the corner of my eye.

"She gets wounded and now she's delusional. When will this end..?"

"I heard that!"

"I know. I meant for you to." He grinned. How annoying. "Look," he said as he put the chair back in the corner of the room. "I'm heading down to the basement now. If you need me, just use the buzzer."

"Hmph." He wants to be a butthead, fine. I turned to my food instead and began eating, not sure if I was really hungry anymore or not. He patted me on the head before turning to walk out. "Hey, I'm not a cat you know! Or a child. People don't pat me on the head!"

"Yeah, yeah, whatever you say." He waved his hand absently as he walked out of my room. *I'll show him.* I devoured the rest of my ramen and cake and downed the can of soda with my pain medicine before he had the chance to make it down to the basement. "I'm done!" I called as I pressed the buzzer by my bed. He walked back into my room with a smirk on his face.

"Ok, no problem. Anything else I can do for you, your highness?"

"No, nothing I can think of. You're free to go," I said with a fake air of superiority that made him chuckle. Maybe he wasn't so bad – when he wasn't fighting the undead and acting like he's always in charge. "Unless you can somehow make me better so I can get back to work today." I knew it was impossible, but a girl could dream.

"Trust me, if I could do that you would've been healed a week ago."

"Oh? And what's that supposed to mean?" If he thought he had it rough, he should try putting himself in my shoes. At least he could still join hunting parties right now, even though he wasn't joining any.

"It's not supposed to mean anything – just that I wish you could've been healed a week ago."

"Why? So you wouldn't have to take care of me anymore?" I knew I was being a pain, but I also knew I didn't want to admit to him I actually enjoyed his company. That would be like admitting that I was letting myself grow attached to someone again – something I constantly reminded myself I couldn't do, no matter how lonely I may feel some days.

"Yeah, that's exactly why."

"Yeah, whatever." I tried not to smile as he put his hands on his hips and gave me an exasperated look.

"Look if I could've, I would have thrown you out of that bed three days ago but no, the doc says you need all the rest you can get and I can't fight the vamps all by myself so it's a catch twenty-two."

"Yeah well, if *I* could help it, I wouldn't have been hurt in the first place! If I wasn't trying to save your sorry little butt…" My voice faded into a mumble. I had opened a can of worms, and I knew it. "I probably wouldn't have been hurt – well, not like that at least."

I had done it now. He was upset. No, he was beyond upset. He was angry now. He narrowed his hazel eyes at me. "I was trying to save *you* from the damn Russian count that you just so happened to be seduced by."

"Hey! I can't help it if all these vampires and such notice how delightful I look. You obviously don't have the brains to." Oops. One thing I should always remember – my temper and my mouth should never go hand in hand, yet they always do.

"Whatever Kel." He threw his arms up into the air. "You've gone loopy since you've been hurt. I'm not going to argue with you." His face was full of scorn when he looked at me again. "Why would I see any of that in such an egotistical little brat like you?"

Ok, now *he'd* done it. "Well, if I'm such an egotistical little brat, why are you still around?"

"Because you're my partner, that's why! And if I'm not going to take care of you who the hell will?"

"I can take care of myself... I *am* seventeen you know." Not like that mattered much – Dustin was only two years older than me.

"Oh, so you'd be happier with me gone then?" He raised an eyebrow at me, as if challenging me.

"I don't know... you've never been gone for me to find out!"

"Fine, what the hell ever. I'm outta here." I watched as he stormed out of my room.

"Ugh! I don't know… maybe I wouldn't be better off..." I mumbled to myself.

"Did you say something?" From the sound of his voice, I can tell he's made it downstairs already. Maybe I could still fix this.

"Yes, and if you'd bring your butt back up here, maybe you could hear me!"

I watched as he stormed back through my door, his jacket and sunglasses on, keys in hand. He stood at the foot of my bed with his arms crossed.

"What is it?" Oh yeah – he's angry.

"I said… Maybe I wouldn't be better off, ok? At least I can admit it though!"

"Oh? And what do you mean by that?" Why couldn't he just let it go? He put his hands on his hips. One of these days my big mouth was going to get me in trouble, I knew it.

"By what? Being able to admit it?"

"Yeah, are you saying I can't admit things?"

"I… didn't say that. Just… other people can't, ok?" I felt my face flush. Yeah, my mouth had just gotten me into trouble once again. I looked up as he let his sunglasses slide down the bridge of his nose to look at me over them. Wow. That was a good look for him. As soon as the thought occurred to me, I blushed even more.

"Whatever, I'm out. I might be back later."

"Yeah, fine." I turned over to face the wall. Maybe he would mistake the red blotches on my face as anger, just as long as I didn't let him see them too well.

"I... ah, forget it." Dustin hesitated. I turned my head to see him stopped at my door.

"What is it?"

He took another step. "It's nothing you want to hear I'm sure."

"And how would you know unless you say it?"

"Because it doesn't matter." I hate it when people do that to me. I wanted to yell at him for it, but with our still very recent arguing in mind, I decided to keep my cool.

"To you, maybe."

"It's something about a person that needs help but hates to get it."

I laid there on my bed as he struggled to continue. Was he talking about me? I had been very independent ever since I lost my parents, and I felt that accepting help would be like showing weakness. Even when the authorities wanted to remove me from my home, I refused so stubbornly that they had to set up someone to come to my house to take care of me, until they finally agreed I was old enough to take care of myself.

"And that same person I kinda care for a lot." He was looking down at his keys. I knew if I didn't lighten the mood, he'd never spit it out.

"Heh, well then I know it's not me."

"Yeah… right." He shook his head. Ok, so maybe I tried lightening the mood because I was afraid of what he might say. That he, what? Cares about me? I was living a doomed life, and I couldn't afford to drag someone else down with me. And I couldn't get attached to him like that. Besides, we were vampire hunters. Partners in a life of hunting the undead. What if one of us died in battle? Having feelings for your hunting partner was always a distraction in a fight, and distractions were dangerous. He glanced out through the doorway, into the hallway.

"I'm gonna take a nap. I'll see you later, ok?" I didn't want to continue the conversation at this point, and it looked like he didn't, either. There was no way he was talking about me, which was for the best anyway.

"Yeah, maybe. I have to go blow off some steam." He turned and walked out. As I heard the front door close, I buried my face into my pillow. Why did I feel disappointed right now? And frustrated?

"Stupid male species! Can't partner up with them, can't strangle them! Ugh!"

As I laid there going over our conversation, the phone rang. I wondered briefly if it could be Dustin, but then thought twice. He hadn't been gone long enough to call already. Well, at least *someone* cared about me. Or it was a call for us to join a hunt. I picked up the phone with at least some pride.

"Hello?"

"Hello there, my darling hunter."

"Wh-who is this?" I didn't have to ask. I would recognize that voice if I heard it in a room full of people screaming bloody murder.

"I think you know very well who this is."

"No, sorry. I guess you have the wrong number, try ag-"

"Look out your window then."

"I can't. My blinds and curtains are closed." The words came out automatically. It wasn't that I couldn't – if I grabbed my crutches and hobbled over to the window, or even hopped on one foot, I could. I just didn't want to. Truth be told, I was scared. I knew I was injured and vulnerable. I could only stand a bit of pressure on my injured ankle still. This was not how I wanted to face this man, of all people.

"You could always open them young hunter. But, perhaps it is better if you don't." I heard the front door open with a creak, and I knew immediately it wasn't Dustin – he always called out the second his head was through the door.

"What do you mean, 'better if I don't?'" The footsteps came up the stairs as I spoke into the telephone. I looked around my room for my closest weapon and found only my crutches. I grabbed for them as my bedroom door slowly opened without a sound. Barely a second passed before I saw one of my crutches flying across the room at my intruder. It was another second before I realized I had thrown it at him and he caught it without a second thought. I felt my heart race as I recognized the danger that was stalking towards me.

"Look hunter, I'm just here to return your cloak. Even I know how much one of these costs." I watched as he casually sauntered to my closet and hung my favorite cloak.

"Is that all?" Skepticism rang in my voice. This was the vampire I'd been hunting. It was during a fight with him that some of his creeps had thrown me into a tree, landing me in my currently disabled mess. It was also the first time I had actually been seriously injured in a fight, which was infuriating. How could I have gotten hurt during a fight with *this* vampire, out of all the vampires I've fought so far?

"Well, no," he chuckled. "I wanted to check on you, of course."

Now I was torn between feeling skeptical and downright incredulous. I'd been hunting this vampire for years, and had come close to actually injuring him during one of the recent fights, and he was here to check on me? When it was one of his goons that did this to me to begin with? Something didn't sound right. "You wanted… to check on me?"

"You know how I feel about you hunter."

"How you… feel?" Maybe it was the pain medication kicking in, but my head felt foggy. This feeling was oddly familiar, although I was unable to place where I had felt it before. As Count Vito stared into my eyes, something clicked. This was how I felt just before I lost all my strength during the last battle and got thrown into the tree. I was not about to let this vampire win the battle I had fought for so long when I couldn't even fight him back. If he was going to kill me, I'd go down fighting. "Listen Count, I've got crutches-" I looked at my one crutch left to me, "er, a crutch, and I know how to use it."

"You won't use it on me." He sounded so sure of himself. It made me want to scream – partly because I knew he was calling my bluff.

"Oh? Are you sure of that?"

"Yes, I am," he stated as he grabbed the one crutch I had left and tossed it towards the door.

I was helpless, which was the worst feeling in the world. Dustin was gone and who knew when he would be back? The vampire that had murdered my family was stalking toward me and I had no escape available.

"What do you want from me?" I tried to scoot further back on my bed.

"You know what I want, my darling little hunter." He was just inches away from me now. I could see his eyes. I had to admit he was really good-looking. Downright hot, actually. He hadn't aged a day since that first night I met him. Wait… vampire. This was not the time to be thinking about that. This was the man I'd promised myself I would hunt down – to avenge my parents.

"No, I don't think I do." *If I could just keep him talking, maybe I could figure something out. Hot. Bad timing! I need to concentrate if I want to live.* Why was it so hard to keep my thoughts straight right now?

"Oh, I think you do. It's the same thing you want," he chuckled as he approached the head of my bed.

"The same thing I want?"

"Remember, I can read your thoughts hunter – I know you have an attraction to me."

"Uh-huh, yeah. And how do you know I'm not somehow attracted to every vampire I meet? Maybe it's just a complex since I hunt your kind so much." *Although I have to admit, he is the best-looking vampire I've met.*

"Why thank you, dear." He chuckled again. Crap – I kept forgetting he could read my thoughts right now, because my defenses were down due to the pain killers. Which meant actually plotting an escape would do me no good. Thoughts kept racing through my mind as he sat on my bed next to me. I could feel my blood pulse as my heart raced. It was as if my body knew that his fangs were about to make contact with my flesh, and it sent a surge of fear and excitement through me at the same time. "I would enjoy nothing more than to bite you. And I know you would enjoy it just as much."

My eyes widened. "No, I wouldn't enjoy it. I don't want to be a vampire – I want revenge on vampires." *Oh my gosh, he's gonna do it. What can I do? I have nowhere to go. But maybe I could let him – no! No way! He may be good-looking, with gorgeous eyes... no, he's a vampire. Stop it!*

"You're afraid, aren't you my dear?" My mind went blank as he ran a long finger up and down my slender neck, his eyes looking directly into mine. All I could think to do was keep him talking.

"S-so what if I am? I'm a mere human. And it isn't every day a human gets bit by a vampire you know."

"Ah, yet it is every day." He traced down my neck once more, going lower to the collar bone, then back up again. My body wouldn't move away from him, despite my desire to be anywhere but here.

"But not every day that a hunter is bitten, right? So it would be natural to be scared – especially if the vampire wanders into her room when she's helpless and can't defend herself."

"That is correct." He smiled a little. It seemed almost sad, like the look of eternal loneliness hid behind that smile. "Do I frighten you?"

I shuddered as he asked that and his finger ran the length of my collar bone again. "Um, a little. Then again, I can't be too scared, because you're-" *Hot. But I shouldn't say that. Then again that could give me a chance to call for help.*

"Little vampire hunter, I do believe you are trying to distract me. Very well then," he laughed. "I shall leave you for now. After all, it is no fun when my target is as completely helpless as you are."

My face flushed with anger. I had nothing but the remote for the TV to throw at him, and I doubted it would do much damage. *Whose fault is it that I'm helpless anyway?*

"Yes," he sighed as he dropped his hand from my collar bone. "I should have kept them under better control. I did tell them not to harm you, but I am sure you understand how it is when you are in a fight – you just do not think things through. He has been… dealt with though."

He hesitated before finishing his sentence. *It sounded like he was about to say killed, which is what Dustin would do if he found this vampire in my room. How long until he gets back, anyway?*

"Yes hunter, he probably would be rather upset if he were to discover my presence in your little… sanctuary. But I suppose that is the power of love, is it not?"

"Yeah, power of..." Wait, did he say *love*? I must've misheard him. Dustin couldn't stand me most days – the only reason he looked after me now was because we were hunting partners. And he definitely had someone else on his mind earlier. "You're crazy."

"Am I? Why don't you take a better look at his eyes one day? You might be surprised." His voice sounded contemptuous.

"I might be surprised, huh?" I looked the count straight in his eyes, as if searching for proof of his falsehoods. He looked smug. Like the cat that trapped the canary, only the canary didn't know it yet. But there was something icy about his look as well. "You've gotta be kidding me, Vamps. Dustin can't stand me."

"If you say so, hunter. Farewell for now. I will be awaiting our next encounter."

"Our next encounter?" *I better be on my feet fighting next time I see him, otherwise I might not be able to resist... no, just go. Walk away before I can't resist despite my best efforts. Damn vampire charms.* With a smile, he nodded and in a puff of smoke vanished, as did the fog in my mind.

I picked up my old teddy bear and took the necklace from around his neck to put on my own. The simple chain contained only a small ring with three hearts on it. My mom had given it to me as a present for my 5th birthday and told me the hearts were each of us: one for Mommy, one for Daddy, and one for me. I grasped the ring and closed my eyes, silently berating myself for having done nothing to this vampire that was supposed to be my target.

Chapter 2

"I'm awake! I was just resting my eyes and…" I bolted into a sitting position before realizing that the sound that had woken me was only Dustin putting my crutches back up against the wall. "Oh," I sighed. "It's you." I took a sip of the soda he must've placed on my nightstand. I felt a serious need for caffeine to wash away the sleep my mind was fighting off right now.

"Uh-huh, sure you were only resting your eyes." He rolled his eyes dramatically. "Look, I'm sorry for earlier."

"Nah, it's my fault. I shouldn't have gotten so upset. I really am sorry, Dustin." *Take a better look at his eyes,* the Count's words echoed again in my head, and I attempted to search Dustin's eyes, and found nothing but a wall. Frustrated with his wall and with myself for getting caught up in such a crazy idea, I sat back in bed and looked toward an actual wall instead.

"So, where did you go, anyway?" He paused before responding.

"What are you looking for, Kel?" Of course my searching hadn't been subtle. I didn't have much experience with that sort of thing. If it wasn't a vampire, I typically wasn't interested in using my energy on it.

I looked back over at Dustin, and his hazel eyes looked clear. Open, as if he had let the wall come down. Could he be opening up to me? The very thought terrified me. No, I cannot let myself get close to anyone.

"Oh, nothing. It's just…" What do I tell him? That the Count was here and said that my partner has feelings for me? Not just any feelings – but *love*? Not even a remote possibility. "Something someone told me once, when I was a kid. Some older guy, and I just wanted to know if he was right, that's all." I looked around my room to distract myself from my lame explanation, and settled my eyes on a shelf that usually held my old teddy bear, now tattered and torn, sitting next to a porcelain doll with visible cracks. The doll had been the last gift my parents brought back for me after a hunting trip. I held onto her so tight while falling asleep as a child, as though she'd somehow bring my parents back. I remember the crushing feeling when she fell out of my bed one night and shattered while I dreamt once again of my parents' deaths.

"Oh, okay." A long pause. "Well, I'm feeling a little uneasy now. I'm sorry."

"Ha, yeah, it's a kind of awkward subject. Of course you'd feel uneasy. You're only human, right?" I forced a small smile. You're only human. It was a longstanding joke between us to remind ourselves that we have limits, and a way to ensure neither of us had been bitten during a fight with vampires. But why does he have that look in his eyes? Like the big brother looking lovingly at his little sister?

"Yeah, and so are you, Kel. Just remember that." A small step backwards. He's about to leave the room, but the question is still itching to be answered. I reached out and grabbed his hand and pulled him to sit on the bed.

"Ok, I can't do this! Listen, I was told by someone, who shall remain completely anonymous, that you…. you like me. Is it true?" My final question came out so fast I wasn't sure it made any sense. It sounded like a jumble in my mind, which was ringing from the blood rushing through my body. *He looks shocked. The Count was wrong.* I knew he would be wrong, so why did I let him get to me?

"Uh… well, of course I like you. You're my partner. I like you as a best friend and someone I would trust my life with. You may be mean sometimes, but you're fair…" His words were slow and measured, which only served to agitate me.

I rolled my eyes, exasperated. This was hard enough already, why did he have to make it harder? "You know what I mean. Like me as more than a partner, or a friend."

"You mean as in lovers?" He shook his head. Just a small shake, but enough for me to see his mind was racing. Probably wondering who would ever say something this crazy to me. If he realizes it was the Count, he'd never trust me again. Just think – a vampire, in the house of a vampire hunting duo, and I did nothing about it. I couldn't, of course, but that didn't make a difference. I looked down to my lap, embarrassed by his phrasing of the question, and for my believing a vampire so easily.

"Yeah, that's, uh, that's one way of saying it." A deep breath. "No matter what your answer is, I can handle it." I kept my head down and did my best to watch him covertly.

Slowly, he closed his eyes and nodded yes. I couldn't believe it! I could barely contain myself as I let out a squeal. "Oh my gosh, that is *so* sweet!" I remembered Count Vito in that moment, and under my breath mumbled, "I can't believe he was right though…" Half lost in my thoughts, I barely noticed Dustin shake his head.

"No, I was agreeing with you that everything would be ok." He stood quickly from the bed. "I… I have to go. I forgot to pick up some things from the supply list."

Oops. Ok, maybe I got too excited. "Ok, we can talk when you get back then! Sorry, I guess the caffeine hit me. Can you pick up some more soda?

"That's fine. I can do that."

"Thank you! How long do you think you'll be gone?" I did my best to temper my smile and excitement at that point.

"I dunno. Probably around thirty minutes to an hour."

"Ok then. Have fun!" I waited until I heard the front door close behind him. I needed someone to talk to, but who? I didn't really have any girlfriends, since most hunters were guys. But I was desperate. Maybe… *Alright, now how do I get ahold of Vito? All these years, it's always been on his terms. Maybe…*

"Hey Vamps! Erm, Count Vito." I was the one needing to talk to him now, so I figured it was best if I probably didn't start the conversation combative. "Where are you? I think we need to talk."

~Not now, dear hunter. You're on your own.~ I jumped at the sound of his voice, realizing it didn't fill the room, only my head.

No other vampire I'd faced had ever been able to get past my defenses. It still bothered me that he could.

"Why?" I looked around my room again, just to be sure he wasn't actually here. "What am I supposed to do? Just let you say and do whatever you want when you decide to come around, and then not be able to reach you when I want to? Some setup that is… You killed my parents, so I have no one else to talk to about this. You owe it to me to show up."

~Not likely, hunter. I'll have you when I choose. You want to talk about your partner? Just tell him how you feel. You already know he likes you. Nothing will come of it unless you tell him you reciprocate.~

"Yeah, but I don't know if I actually like him like that. I just think it's sweet that he likes me. And no, you cannot have me when you choose," I said as his other words registered in my mind. "Maybe I'll find a way to make it where you'll never be able to have me by your side." *Although it's not like I could have anyone by my side until I kill you anyway. I can't lose anyone else.*

~That's not likely, dear. You do seem quite interested in him, though, so you should proceed with caution. He's simply afraid of his feelings. He has not accepted his feelings for you as I have mine.~

"Look, I can't do this. When I talk to people, or vampires in this case, I prefer to talk face to face. To know where the voice is coming from."

~Dah, very well then, my dear.~

In a poof, he appeared in my bedroom. A part of me was always terrified when I saw him here. Although I've spent the last two years hunting him, I had failed to actually locate him. We had finally located his castle in a forest surprisingly close by, but he was never there when we went hunting him. Yet, over the years, I would sense he was here. Or I'd wake up in the night to see his silhouette. It was probably stupid of me to live in the same house since becoming a vampire hunter. It was never smart for your prey to know where you lived. Where you were most vulnerable.

"No need to be scared, my dear. I will not harm you. I promised to watch over you, and I keep my promises. So, what was it you wanted to discuss? Ah yes, your… partner and him being afraid of his feelings for you." There was a hint of disdain in his voice as he sat on the edge of my bed. My legs twitched at his closeness. This vampire I swore to destroy, so close, and by my own choosing. My own invitation. And the fight inside of me to try to kill him now or to wait and listen to him. With a sigh, he placed a hand to his temple and continued. "You tire me, hunter, and I have a headache."

"I tire you? Guess I do my job well, then. Why is he afraid of his feelings?" I hated myself for this. This man – no, this vampire – and the conflicted relationship I had with him. He was my enemy. He killed my parents. However, I also felt a sense of protection when he was around. Like he would protect me from all dangers, if I'd allow him. But he was a danger. How could he protect me from himself?

"Yes, you tire me. He is afraid that if he loves you, it will compromise your teamwork and your friendship. I know your feelings for him are rather complicated, too. However, you also should know that I desire you to be my bride. This little game of ours, though, is on my terms, not yours."

"Your bride as in a victim? Or something else?" I shouldn't push him. I know I shouldn't. I couldn't help it, though. Since that night, twelve years ago, I've never been able to stop wondering why he didn't just kill me. Was he unable to? I remembered a time when I was around 12, I had woken in the middle of the night and saw his silhouette sitting at the edge of my bed, just like now. And my mind, still dazed from sleep, found the courage to ask why he had killed my parents.

I had heard the story from other hunters growing up. They had been vampire hunters, too. They were paid to hunt top tier vampires, called elite vampires, because they were some of the best there were. I remember being so proud of them. However, the last job they received was to hunt Count Vito. No one had ever seen him unless he allowed it. My parents had gotten close to locating him, and he knew it. So he followed them and killed them that very night. I never got an answer as to why he killed my parents and didn't kill me. He never spoke of that night, even when I asked him. He must've known I'd grow to be a vampire hunter like my parents, and that I'd want my revenge. It just made no sense to leave me alive.

"No, dearest, you are more than just a meal. However, I don't feel hungry at the moment, so that could always change." There was a glint of humor in his eyes. A vampire with a dark sense of humor. Great.

"Ok, next question then: what are the terms to your little game?" I released my chocolate brown hair from the ponytail it had been in all day, allowing it to fall to the middle of my back. The stress of the day was getting to me, and my head began pounding. I ran my fingers through my hair a few times while I waited for an answer. Again I saw a glint in his eyes, this time accompanied by a smirk.

"When you fall into my traps is when we play. I will have you, hunter Kel. However, that's not what is most pressing."

"Then what is?"

"Destroying the one thing your friend holds dearest of all."

"And what's that?" I looked at him, apprehensive and confused. As far as I knew, what Dustin held dearest of all was hunting vampires. How exactly did this Count plan to take that from him?

He placed his hand on my leg, which sent shivers through my body. "His love for you."

My mouth fell open as I let out a short breath. *Does he really believe Dustin loves me that much? And if he's right, how would this vampire take that love from him? He couldn't. Could he?*

"I can. And I have already started. You will not win, hunter. He is ready to tell you everything about how he feels. The question is will you be the one to destroy his feelings by denying what he hopes for, and what you want, because of your fears?"

"Wha… what are you talking about?" I didn't like where this conversation was going. *This was a mistake, I knew it. And my closest weapon is across the room, while I'm stuck here on the bed, injured, and with Vito's hand on my leg, reminding me I can't make a move without alerting him. Why did I think this was a good idea?*

"Yes, I have worn out my welcome. You'll want to call on me again though. But for now, I leave you." With a snap of his fingers, he was gone.

I hardly had a chance to process the fact that Vito was gone as quick as he had arrived when I heard the front door open. "I'm back!" came the familiar voice of my partner from downstairs. Oh crap. My head snapped up at the sound of Dustin's voice.

"Hey! Welcome back!" I called out to him. I tried to keep my voice as normal as I could, but my heart was pounding like it did in a fight. Only there wasn't a single undead around now for me to focus my energy on. I heard him put a few things away before coming up the stairs and peeking into my room.

"So… how was your trip to the store?" *More enjoyable and relaxing than my time, I hope.*

"It was fine. I got what you asked for." He definitely seemed… maybe not more relaxed, but definitely not angry, for now at least. He smiled an awkward smile.

"Thank you." I smiled back. "Listen, I'm sorry. You've been nice and helpful while I've been recovering and I've been nothing but mean, haven't I?"

He nodded slowly. Probably caught off guard or thought I was setting a trap for him. "Ok, I won't lie. You have been pretty crabby at times, yes. But I haven't really been that nice, either."

"You've been nicer than me. There's gotta be a way I can make it up to you, isn't there? I feel bad."

"Don't worry about it, Kel. It's fine. It's not easy being hurt and out of action."

"It doesn't matter. I shouldn't treat you like that."

He sighed and shrugged his shoulders. "Maybe." He sat at the edge of my bed. The same spot Vito had been sitting a few minutes before. The very thought made me tense up just a little. "What's wrong?" Dustin looked at me with concern in his eyes and a knowing look. He always knew when something was bothering me. I was terrible at hiding it.

"Wrong? Nothing. I've just been thinking, that's all." I pulled my hair back into my usual ponytail. I desperately needed something to do with my hands.

"Something is the matter, Kel. What is it?"

"Nothing, really. There's just been a lot to think about lately, ya know?" I forced a smile and hoped with all my might that it looked natural.

"Yeah, I know that feeling. I've been doing a lot of thinking, too."

Was I ready for this conversation? *No. I can't let it happen. We're vampire hunters. And I've lost too many people already. Loved ones. I can't love until I know it's safe.* "Well, it's been a long day. I guess I should let you get to sleep."

He stared at me for a good minute. Maybe more. It felt like five minutes, at least. It was like time slowed down to draw out my agony. "I can stay for a while and talk, if you want."

"Umm… yeah. No. Ugh, I don't know." I buried my face in my hands before pulling them down off my face. "It's just… an old friend of mine called today, while you were out. She wanted my advice on something that I have no idea how to help her with, and it's really bugging me. She said she kinda likes two guys, and she's pretty sure they both also like her. But she wasn't sure who she should go for, and I had no idea what to tell her. Does that even make any sense? I mean, what should I even tell her?"

He sat there for a moment, considering the situation. Was I being too obvious? Could he tell I had made up a cover story to try to not be caught?

"Well, which one does she like the most?"

"She's not sure."

"Ok, which one has the better qualities?"

"She didn't really say…" *Better qualities? One is safe, one is dangerous and safe at the same time. Both are good looking. One is my fight partner, and the other… I'm hunting to kill. But I don't know if I'll ever manage it. And then I'll be obsessed over him my whole life, afraid to let anyone get close to me.* His next words brought me out of my racing thoughts.

"Ok then, I would say this: if I were her, I would go with the one who makes me feel the most comfortable and safe, and also if he can be there for me when I need him to be. One that understands me and knows how to help me and also himself when needed. He should be somewhat romantic, charming, and funny. And definitely caring. That's what every girl I've known has always liked most."

I nodded along as he listed qualities. I had never thought about these things. Seventeen years old, and I'd never had a real relationship. I had always been too afraid, because of the Count.

"Sorry, I guess she was so confused that she's got me all confused, too." I chuckled. "She did say that one is more romantic in a weird sort of way, but the other one is a bit shy."

"And why is he shy?"

"She doesn't know. I guess he wouldn't tell her." *Why ARE you so shy about this, Dustin? You like me, so why not tell me?*

"Well, if he really likes this girl, why doesn't he just tell her?"

"Because he's too shy?"

"Unless he's not sure if she likes him back?"

"Oh. I suppose that *could* be it."

"Well, it could be that, at least. Maybe she needs to start off by telling him how she feels, and see what he says." He yawned and I smiled at him. He really was a great partner and friend.

"Come here," I pulled him into a hug. "Thank you, for all your help."

"You're welcome, Kel. As much as we fight, you are my best friend."

"And you're mine, too. And I'll admit it – I'm grateful for that."

He chuckled softly. "Well, that seems like the start to many bold and new things." He stood up and I softly repeated his words to myself. "Yes, bold and new. You've admitted something to me for the first time tonight. Good night, Kel. I'll see you some time in the morning."

"Y-yeah. Goodnight, Dustin." *What exactly did I admit to him? I'm awful at lying, so maybe he knew the whole time I made it up? And why won't he just admit his feelings to me? And not deny it right after? And how could I tell him that I actually like him without him putting his walls up again? Then, of course, there are the reasons for my fear of a relationship...*

Chapter 3

I let out my breath in a huff. That hurt. My ribs were getting better, but still sore. I couldn't sleep. I kept replaying the conversations I'd had with both the Count and Dustin. And I felt impossibly lost. My insides were twisting to resemble my emotions: desire to kill the Count, but also a feeling of… affection towards him? And I knew I cared for Dustin, but in what way? Did it even matter? I had been so excited that Dustin might like me that I had almost forgotten myself completely. After the one person I had gotten close to after my parents' death was also killed by a vampire, I swore not to get close to anyone until I had completed my mission. And I've been proud to be able to keep to that promise. Until now.

"No… stop… get away… No! KEL!!!"

Dustin's voice rang loud from his room. I hobbled as quickly as I could across the hall to his bedroom. As I opened the door, I could hear him saying "it was a dream. Only a dream."

"Dustin? Are you ok?"

He looked up at me as I turned on the light, still trying to catch his breath, his face dripping with sweat. I'm sure he could see the worry written all over my face as his wiped the sweat from his.

"Yeah, I just had a bad dream, that's all. I didn't mean to wake you."

"It's ok. I wasn't sleeping. Are you sure you're ok?"

He ran his hand through his hair, which was wet with sweat, and took a few steadying breaths. "Yeah, I'm ok. Just shaken, that's all. And I thought nightmares were for little kids." He let out a soft, curt laugh.

"Not at all. Even as we get older, our subconscious thoughts still plague us." I thought of my recurring nightmare. The night my parents were killed. The memory still plagued me. "You gonna be ok? I mean, you don't need me to sing you to sleep or anything, right?"

He chuckled at my childish jab. "I guess you're right. And thanks, but I'll be ok. I'm going downstairs for a bit. You need anything?"

"No, I'm fine. I'm gonna head back to bed." He nodded. I could tell the nightmare was still bothering him. I wonder if he knew he called out my name? "Good night, Dustin. And, uh… sweet dreams, ok?"

"I'll try." I went back to my room as I heard him softly thud, thud, thud down the steps. Back in my room, I laid down on my bed and stared up at the blank ceiling and fought with myself. I wanted to sleep, and I knew I needed to in order to heal faster. But talking about nightmares and remembering the night of my parents' death? I knew if I slept now, I'd be the next one with nightmares. I listened instead to the sounds of Dustin in the kitchen.

The freezer door opened, and a soft thud of something on the table. An empty bowl with a spoon in it. Ice cream. Not a bad way to console oneself after a particularly nasty nightmare. A little bit later, the water running. The bowl and spoon put in the dish drainer. And then the soft thuds of his feet on the staircase coming back up. My door slowly opened. My breath caught. Why was I afraid now that it may have been the Count instead of Dustin?

"Is that you, Dustin?"

"You should be asleep, Kel. Do you know what time it is? You know you're not going to get any better by staying up all night."

"No, I actually have no idea what time it is. I just… can't sleep, that's all."

"What's the matter, Kel?"

"Insomnia?"

Dustin crossed his arms over his bare chest and raised an eyebrow at me. "I don't think so. You can sleep pretty soundly just about anytime, anywhere."

I couldn't help but notice how muscular his chest was in the soft moonlight coming in from my window. Fighting vampires was exhausting work, but it definitely kept us both in good shape.

"What's wrong," he asked, "something on your mind?"

"I guess so. I'm just..." terrified of having nightmares? No, can't tell him that. "Not used to being injured this bad. A couple of days I can handle. This is too much. I feel like hunting down a vampire right now, but I can't. It's not fair."

He chuckled softly. It was a nice sound. Much better than the terrified scream less than half an hour ago. "I understand that feeling. You'll be well enough in a week or so. Probably. Maybe sooner," he added as my eyebrows shot up into my forehead.

"I can't handle another week or so of this. I want to be better now. Tonight. I want to go hunt vampires!"

I was sounding like a whiny brat, and I knew it. I couldn't help it, though. It was easier to play it off as my injuries keeping me awake, rather than admitting the truth. That I was terrified of my nightmares. But also… I was terrified of the end of my nightmare. Every time the Count put me back to bed and said he'd protect me. And I looked forward to the end of the nightmare every time.

"I know, Kel. I want you better, too. I miss having the Kel that's on the up and up, kicking some vampire butt. Really though, you should be fine in a couple more days."

"Yeah, but I miss being on the up and up, too."

"Get some sleep, ok?" He turned toward the door. But I didn't want to be alone right now. I was scared of looking forward to the end of my nightmare once again. A vampire hunter shouldn't look forward to a vampire telling her he'd protect her.

"Hey, Dustin? You mind sitting in here and just… talking? I mean, it's not a good night of sleep for either of us anyway, right?" He pulled the chair from the corner of my room to sit closer to me.

"You know," I sighed, "I don't know about you, but I'd really rather be out hunting one vampire in particular right now… Count Vito."

"Yeah, I want him, too." Dustin knew that Vito killed my parents. He didn't know about the Count promising to protect me, though. I could never bring myself to tell anyone about that.

"I still can't believe his goons got me. I guess I was being careless, huh?"

"Nah, you were watching my back. I'm glad you were there, or I would've been killed. I am sorry you got hurt on my part, though."

"That's what partners are for, right?"

"Yeah, you're right. Just let me take the next time, though?" He smiled sarcastically and winked.

"What, and let *you* take all the credit? I think not." He laughed and brushed a few strands of hair away from my face.

"Thanks, partner. I owe you a lot."

"Yeah, I'm sure you'll find a way to make it up to me." I laughed a nervous laugh. His face was close, and I could see his eyes looking directly back into mine, despite the low light. They were a clear hazel tonight, not cloudy like they sometimes got when he was upset.

"I'm sure I will one of these days." Then he blinked and looked away, shifting his body further away, mumbling under his breath "the closer you come, the weaker I get…"

"If it ain't happenin' now, it just ain't happenin' yet. I know that song. It's a good one." I smiled sadly. I knew the song well, and it wasn't a happy one. "Tell me what's bothering you?"

"It's nothing real important. Not really much to tell."

"Then why do I get the feeling that whatever it is that's bothering you is the same thing you were having a nightmare about?"

"No, not at all. It was just a dream about a dear friend of mine being bitten, and I couldn't do anything but watch in horror."

"Oh. That *is* a nightmare." *He called out my name. He dreamt I was being bitten. No wonder it bothers him – it's a real possibility in our line of work.*

"I'm sorry," I said with a sigh. "I shouldn't have pestered you about it. I'll let you go and sleep now. I promise I'll try to sleep too."

"Ok, I will." He smiled an awkward smile before adding "g'night, Kel," and trudging off to his room. I could've sworn I heard him still singing the same song on his way out, though.

* * * * *

The next morning, I decided to wake up early. I thought about the previous night, and how I practically ran into Dustin's room when he called out my name. I gingerly set my feet on the floor and was pleasantly surprised by the lack of pain in my ankle. Now if only my ribs would heal as fast. I put on a set of fresh clothing and decided to go downstairs and cook some real food for breakfast. Dustin and I had agreed long ago I'd do the cooking. I wasn't a master chef, but anything I made was definitely better than what he could make. I heard the shower running as I walked past the bathroom to go downstairs to the kitchen. As I finished up with my cooking, I heard Dustin from the base of the stairs.

"Well good morning."

"Hey, good morning. Have a seat, breakfast is ready. We've got scrambled eggs, bacon cooked just the way you like it, and waffles."

"Wow, that's amazing." A smile. A genuine smile. I haven't seen one of those since right before the fight that ended with my injury.

"Yeah, I thought I'd do something nice for a change." I laughed.

"Well, ok then. Do you need a hand?"

"Nope. This is your morning to relax. You've been taking care of me since the fight. Now it's my turn to repay you."

"Relax… that would be good." He took a seat at the kitchen table and cracked his neck. "Now if only someone could tell my shoulders that."

With a smile I placed breakfast on the table and began to massage his shoulders. He was definitely tense and carried more stress than he let on. He began to relax a little before pulling away quickly and turning to face me.

"It's ok, Kel. I got it. Thanks anyway, though."

He is so stubborn, I thought with a grin. "Just relax. We both work hard, and you deserve this once in a while. My mom took massage therapy when she had spare time. She was always massaging my dad's shoulders, and taught me a few things early on."

"It sure feels that way." I began to massage down his back, surprised at just how tight his muscles were. He was definitely carrying a lot of stress. But when I got to his lower back, I stopped abruptly.

~Uh-uh, my darling hunter. That's where you stop.~

"You ok?"

"Yeah… just hungry. My stomach just growled. We should eat, before the food gets too cold."

~Good choice, hunter.~

Yeah, not like I had much choice. I remember the last boyfriend I tried to have. I sat at the table across from Dustin. Although Vito could truly claim he hadn't killed my almost boyfriend, I knew one of his underlings had. *'I'll protect you, and your innocence, until the day you are mine.' I remember. You'll die before that happens, Count.*

It was middle school, when I had my first crush. The boy was a year older than me, and tried to convince me to skip class to go make out. That's the first time I remember hearing Vito's voice in my head directly. I had recognized his voice when he said he would protect me and my innocence, of course, but couldn't find a source outside of my head. I was so shaken up, I didn't talk to my crush again for a whole day. He thought I was mad at him, but how could I explain that I was hearing the voice of a vampire in my head? I thought I was going crazy at the time.

~We shall see, my dear. You will be mine, hunter.~

"Kel? What's wrong?"

I snapped my head up to look at Dustin, staring at me with worry all over his face. No. I couldn't let the same thing happen to him. I wasn't sure why Vito hadn't killed him already, since he knew where we live. I knew if I let myself feel anything more for my partner before killing Vito, he would end up the same as my first crush. I felt shame – I couldn't even bring myself to think of his name. He died, all because I had dared to have feelings for him.

"Nothing. I was just thinking. After breakfast, I want to start training again. Slowly," I added, before he could swallow the bite of food in his mouth and protest. "My ankle is feeling better. I don't want to lose more strength than I already have."

He swallowed and eyeballed me. "Light training only. Your ribs-"

"Are still killing me, I know. I won't push it. I just need something…" *To keep my mind off of you. Off of… him.* "…to keep me occupied. I'm bored without training."

A few more bites of food and he finally agreed. After breakfast we went to the basement where the training area was set up. It felt good to be back in there. After a few warmup stretches I felt ready to go. Walking laps around the room felt good, so I did some ballet to test my limits, followed by deeper stretches. A few modified pushups though, and the pain got worse. I looked over at Dustin, who was practicing his sparring, dripping in sweat. I'd get there again, though it felt like it'd never happen.

"I'm going to go shower and watch some TV." He nodded as I walked up the steps. On the way out, I stopped and grabbed a dagger to put under my pillow. I didn't want to be caught vulnerable like that again. In the shower, with warm water running from my hair down my spine, I allowed myself to cry a little. I cried from frustration – not being able to train, not being able to love without fear, and not being able to entirely hate with every fiber of my being the vampire that started this whole mess.

Finally feeling somewhat better, I finished my shower, got dressed, and went downstairs to watch TV. Maybe the change of scenery would help. I didn't even realize I had dozed off until Dustin covered me with a blanket. "Dustin?" He turned back to face me, hair still damp from his shower. "Stay with me?"

A small nod and he sat on the sofa next to me. Some cheesy movie was on, but he didn't bother to change it. I dozed a little longer. When I awoke a few hours later, Dustin was asleep next to me. Seemed like the lack of sleep the night before and then training took its toll on both of us. I ran my fingers through his hair a few times, then kissed him gently on his slightly parted lips, before pulling away quickly. His eyes fluttered open. Did he catch me? Even worse… did *he* know? I hadn't thought about it before acting. Maybe we were safe.

"Kel? What happened? I fell asleep?"

Good, he didn't ask about…. that. "Yeah, but it's fine." *Maybe one kiss wouldn't hurt…*

The phone rang. Perfect timing, of course. I picked up the phone sitting on a table next to the sofa. "Yeah?"

"Hello, my little hunter."

My eyes widened. The Count had only called that one time, and even then it was only because he wanted something and I was hurt. "H-hello. What do you want?"

"Who is it?" Dustin sat next to me and whispered. I simply mouthed the name Vito. I felt his body go rigid next to mine. Vito hadn't called when Dustin was around last time, and I hadn't told him about it. Dread began to fill me.

"So, how is Dustin? And the kiss? Did you enjoy it?"

"Good. And yes." Deep breaths. I couldn't afford to let either of them hear my panic. I was met with a chuckle coming from the receiver.

"Good, because that shall be your last."

"What makes you say that?"

"I'll wait no longer. Tonight, you will become mine. When Dustin is away, I shall take you."

Click. I stared blankly ahead and listened to the dial tone for a moment before realizing exactly what he had said and slowly hanging up the phone.

"Kel? What is it? What did he say? How did he get the phone number?"

"Dustin, please don't leave me." I looked at him with pleading eyes. I couldn't face the Count alone on a good day, and right now I was still hurting and my mind was still a jumble trying to figure out my own emotions. I'd have no chance of fighting him off. I needed my partner, and would just have to accept the fact that I was vulnerable right now.

"Shhh, I'm here. It's ok." He held me close as I started sobbing like a baby. I felt weak and vulnerable. I hated feeling those things. I felt his lips kiss the top of my head and I silently sobbed a little more. "He's playing mind games with you, Kel."

"Maybe you're right," *but mind games are his specialty*, I thought to myself.

"Of course I'm right. I won't let anything happen to you." I looked up at him, hopeful. "Now you see? That's the Kel I know. The one with confidence and hope. And of course, always a gleam of 'I'm going to kick your ass' in her eye."

I laughed. He was right – this wasn't like me. The youngest person to ever graduate vampire training school at barely age fifteen, I was confident and always ready to kick some vampire fangs out. Then again, the Count didn't often reveal himself to me, until more recently. Instead, he often avoided me since I graduated. Always lurking nearby, I was sure. Like I could feel his presence watching me, but never had he directly threatened to take me away. He knew my goal. It was these new actions that made me feel nervous. I felt Dustin run his fingers down my spine and arched my back. My downfall is that I'm ticklish. He stopped as he felt me press against him.

"You did that on purpose, didn't you?" I raised my eyebrows at him.

"Of course," he chuckled. "How else was I going to get you out of your head there?"

"Ok then, just for that…" I gave him a devious smile and started to tickle him back. Living with someone meant learning a lot about them, and I happened to know Dustin was just as ticklish as I was.

"Ok, ok," he breathed between bouts of laughter, "you win." I stopped and laughed. "At least you're smiling again."

"Thanks," I took a few breaths. "It's getting late, but I don't want to be alone. Will you lay with me for a little while? Please?"

His eyebrows shot up. "Yeah, of course."

Up in my room, we laid on my bed. My mind was finally calming down, allowing me to drift off to sleep, when Dustin's cell phone rang from his room.

"Hang on, I'll be right back," he assured me as he kissed me on the forehead. He was being extra affectionate tonight, and I wasn't sure if I liked it or if it worried me. A few seconds later, I heard his voice from his bedroom.

"Hello? What?? No! I'll be right there, hold on!"

"Dustin?" I called out to him as I got up out of bed. "Who was it?"

Moments later, he reappeared in my doorway. "Kel, I have to go. I'm sorry. My family is in trouble, the whole town is being overrun."

"Go. They need you right now." It killed me that I couldn't help him, but I also knew not to offer. He'd refuse because I was still on the mend. With tears in his eyes, he crossed my room quickly and embraced me. I felt the fear radiating from his whole body.

"I'll be back, I promise."

"I know." One last look at me – was that really fear in his eyes? – and he raced out the door. Within minutes he had gathered his weapons, bolted out the door into the car, and was gone. Just like that. It only took a few minutes longer for me to decide I couldn't just sit still. *A battle like that will leave him hungry. Let's see what I can cook up for him to eat when he gets back.* At the base of the stairs, I turned left toward the kitchen when I heard a knock on the door and changed course, going straight to the door instead.

"Hello?" I spoke as I opened the door. My eyes widened in dismay as I saw him standing there – the one and only Count Vito. How could I have forgotten what he had just told me on the phone earlier? Wearing dress slacks, a royal blue button up shirt with a jacket with tails and a cape, he looked like he was going to some sort of a fancy party. My surprise at his appearance, however, was my downfall. It took only that split second for him to have a grip on my mind as I felt the fog fill my brain. I normally tried to have my mental wall up, but the Count had known me since before I learned those defenses, so even as I learned how to block him out, he always found a way to get past my walls. I always had to be prepared for a mental fight to keep my wits about me if he was around, and if I didn't put up my extra defenses quick enough, it could mean game over for me.

"Hello there," he said with a glint in his eyes. I couldn't think properly, and all I could manage was to slam the door in his face.

"Go away," I yelled through the door. I was fighting to get my defenses in place, which was hard with the fog already filling my mind and making it hard to think straight. My favorite dagger was downstairs in the basement, and with my having to fight for mental clarity, it would make for a really tough physical battle.

~You will open the door.~

"No, I… I won't. I can't…" I found myself opening the door a crack, despite telling myself not to. This was the true power of an elite vampire. They didn't win over their victims with force. They used mind games, making it nearly impossible for a victim to think clearly about escape or protection. That was exactly why mental defenses were one of the first lessons taught in a vampire hunter school, though that lesson never seemed to matter when it came to my defenses against Vito.

~Open the door and let me in, dear hunter.~

Every fiber of my being screamed no, and yet I found myself opening the door fully, allowing this deadly vampire to pass into my sanctuary once again.

~Allow me to enter.~

I tried not to. I tried to stand my ground, but found myself stepping back. *Defenses*, I told myself. *Defenses, now!* I heard the Count chuckle. These must be the games he spoke of. The ones we'd play on *his* terms. He closed the door behind him. He took hold of my chin and tilted my head up. I hadn't realized just how small I was compared to him, but noted now that he was at least a head taller than I was. He slowly lowered his head to mine, and pressed his lips to my lips.

~Kiss back, my dear.~ I couldn't resist. I couldn't seem to get my defenses in place. He began to run a finger down the side of my face, along my neck, and finally to my collarbone. I tilted my head down and looked away from him.

"Why deny what you want?"

"I… don't know." I still couldn't quite think straight, but the fog was clearing some.

"You know I want you, my dear hunter. And I know you want me by your side."

"Yes, I do." *Why did I say that? I didn't want to say that.* And yet, an air of truth rang around the sentence.

"Then it shall be done tonight. You come with me now." He hugged me tight. Not an embrace meant to keep me from running. It felt more like a hug from a dear loved one that thought they may never see you again. He stepped back and looked at me, as I stood there in my normal spaghetti strap shirt and pants. The outfit was my go-to as it was comfortable and didn't leave a lot of excess material in my way during a fight. I noted how vastly different our appearances were. He was well put together, and I stood here looking like a very average teenager. I felt the fog clear just a bit more. "You are very beautiful, hunter."

There it was! My head finally cleared enough to put my defenses in place and start thinking clearly. I cocked my head at him. "That's what *all* the vampires say, you know. Right before they try to kill me, that is."

He chuckled. "I see you broke through the spell. Your skills are getting better with each passing day. No worries. You will still come with me tonight, however it will be of your own accord now. I will enjoy it, either way."

"I'm sure you would. Sorry to be the bearer of bad news, but I'm not going anywhere with you, *Count*. You want to whisk me away... for what? To make me some vampire bride? I hate vampires and hunt your kind. What sort of a vampire do you think I'd make?"

"It wouldn't matter. Once you become one of us, I can make you forget the painful memories that fuel your hatred. Just think: no painful memories of your childhood, no sorrow, no illness. No more nightmares."

"No more nightmares?" I had never considered there could be an upside to becoming a vampire. But the possibility of no more nightmares was actually causing me to considerate it. *I could forget all of the pain, all of the horrible memories. But...*

"Do I tempt you with my offer?" There was a gleam in his eye. The look one gets when playing chess, knowing they just cornered their opponent into check, with very few options left.

"I am tempted, but..."

"But...?"

"Dustin." He grimaced at the name. "You have to promise me that you will leave Dustin alone if I agree to come with you."

There was a fire in his eyes as he stared at me. A cold fire, like a mixture of jealousy and intent to murder. "It doesn't matter what happens to him, hunter. You are coming with me either way."

"But if you promise that, I will go with you willingly. I won't fight you. Isn't that a better prize than a forced bride?"

He paused for a moment, thinking it over. "Very well, my dear. I will spare his life."

"And his family?"

"Yes, their lives as well."

"Then it's a deal. I need a moment to pack some things..."

"I have all you will ever need. We leave now to your new home."

"I need to bring one thing with me. Please," I implored. "It's important to me."

He agreed and I ran to my room. I wrote a scribbled note telling Dustin I had gone with Vito to save his family, and not to worry. I grabbed my old, tattered teddy bear with my necklace around his neck and returned to the Count. "Ok," I said, holding back my tears. "I'm ready."

He gazed down momentarily at my teddy bear with recognition showing in his eyes, and didn't seem surprised by my choice. Did he remember handing me my teddy bear that night when I was a child? He wrapped his arms around me and snapped his fingers with a flourish. In an instant, we appeared inside his castle.

Chapter 4

"Welcome to your new home."

I raised my eyebrows incredulously. "You don't do much decorating, do you? This place seriously needs an overhaul."

As I entered the castle, I noticed a few doors off to either side, with a grand staircase on the left side of the balcony of the second floor, flowing down like the ones you'd see in old movies. The walls were sparsely decorated, and most of the décor was definitely over a hundred years old. It was mostly a few vases that sat empty on pedestals. I noted that oddly, I didn't see any portraits. The only painting I noticed was of a country landscape, with green rolling hills and a hint of wind blowing the grass.

"Maybe a woman's touch." It was ironic to hear those words coming from my mouth, since I didn't really have a lot of interior decorating knowledge myself.

"I resent that remark, however I will admit it has been a while since a charming woman has dwelled in these halls, and I've little time or reason to consider the décor for the past couple of decades."

"Oh? And how long has it been since a woman lived here?" I gave him a suspicious look. It seemed as though I may not be the first "bride" he had chosen in his undead life. And who knows? Maybe I could annoy him into changing his mind and letting me leave.

"That really is none of your business, my dear."

I sauntered over, allowing my hips to sway as womanly as I could. Time to turn on the charm and find out exactly what I was up against. "Oh, dear Count, I think it is my business, if I'm to live here together with you. You should be able to tell me anything, right?"

He allowed a small smirk before answering. "Almost a hundred years. Ninety-eight long, cold years of being alone."

Ouch. I wasn't expecting it to be that long. That was an entire lifetime, if you were lucky enough to live a really long life. "Well, you're going to need a major redecorating job if I'm gonna be living here for who knows how long."

"Of course, my dear hunter. Whatever you would like, I'm sure my servants can help you. Shall I show you to your chambers now?"

"Whatever you wish, my dear Count," I replied with a smile. Granted, it was an obviously fake smile, but I had to buy myself some time to figure out a plan from here. I followed him up the great staircase to one of the upper floor areas, and felt the entire time a conflicting feeling, like I didn't belong here in these walls, but was also right where I was supposed to be. But I knew I definitely didn't fit in here, in this building that seemed as ancient as the Count must've been. *Come to think of it, I don't even know how old he is.*

"Here are you chambers," he said as he opened the door. "I do believe you will like it. To your right you have a master closet, which I imagine to be around the size of your former bedroom. Try on any garment you like. They should all fit and they are all yours."

I peeked into the "closet" that was definitely as big as my bedroom back home, if not bigger. It was filled with a wide variety of clothes: shirts of varying sleeve lengths and colors, pants in varying styles, skirts of varying lengths and colors, and dresses. A lot of dresses. There was also a wide variety of shoes: some sneakers, but mostly heels and other dress shoes to match the dresses hanging above them. I had never seen so many different clothes all in one place. The variety was even greater than what I had seen in a store.

"For tonight's event, I request that you wear the one laid out for you." He gestured toward a chair in the closet.

"Oh my gosh, what a beautiful dress! And red is one of my best colors. Made from velvet? This is amazing, and…" I stopped myself short. What was I doing? I had fantasized about the times my mother would dress me fancy for evening gatherings, but it had never happened, and never would because of this man right here. I cleared my throat.

"Thank you." My mother was big about manners before she had died, and taught me to be courteous to everyone, especially if they showed me a kind gesture.

"You're welcome, my dear." A small smile. I just gave him the upper hand, and worse yet was that he knew it, and so did I.

"Well, out you go if I'm going to try it on." I waved him away.

"Of course," he chuckled. "I wouldn't want to tarnish this moment by watching you dress."

I watched as he left the room, and locked the door behind him. I didn't think it would make much of a difference though. I placed my old teddy bear on the chair and picked up the dress. It was soft and had boning in it to accentuate my figure. Though I wasn't like most teenage girls in many ways, I was exactly like them when it came to dresses with one big difference: I had never owned a nice dress. Why would I? I spent all of my time hunting vampires, not going to parties. A dress just wasn't feasible in my lifestyle.

I changed into the dress and put on the matching shoes and jewelry before looking into the mirror. I almost couldn't believe it was me looking back. My shoulders were bare as the dress had no straps, and it showed me a figure I didn't even know I had, with a slit going to my thigh on my right leg. The heels had rhinestones over the toes and around the ankle strap. It took me a good minute or so to even admit to myself that it was, indeed, me staring back from the mirror. I stepped out of the closet and came face to face with the Count, and waited for his response.

"Well? What do you think?"

"You look simply ravishing, my dear."

"I know," I said with a wink and a smile.

A small chuckle. So much for trying to annoy him. Part of me was ok with that, though. *Why is it so easy to joke with him?* He called for a servant who came in and fixed my hair into a cascade of curls. A far cry from the functional ponytail I normally fashioned.

"Shall we begin tonight's activities?" He offered an arm.

"I'll admit, I am a little nervous." *If it weren't for the fact that I know how much danger I'm in right now, this could feel downright magical.*

"Let me help you with that, my dear." He led me to a chair in my personal sitting room and sat me down, gathering my curls and placing them to the side. Was he going to change me now? I felt my whole body go stiff at the very thought. "Just relax," he said as he began to massage my bare shoulders. I stiffened even more. I don't know what I had really expected by agreeing to come here, but a back massage definitely didn't make the list.

"I am trying to help you, my dear. Your muscles are rock solid," he said as he slid his hands away from my neck and down my shoulders. "That's not healthy for such a young girl."

I turned my head slightly to look over my shoulder, recognizing that with his hands just below my shoulders, I was truly trapped where I was. "What did you expect? I'm a vampire hunter, not some spoiled princess."

"Ah, but you will soon be a countess, living a life of luxury."

"Like that's going to be any easier?" I scoffed, then drew a sharp breath as I felt him lean close to my ear.

"Yes, it is," he whispered before placing a soft kiss on my neck, giving me chills.

There came a knock on the door. "Enter," he said curtly. A young-looking man came in and began speaking to Vito. Something about a village, and the attacking vampires have returned to their homes. "You may go," he spoke simply and the other vampire left. The Count turned back to me.

"As promised, your… partner and his family are safe. Their village is no longer under siege."

It took me a moment to process it. The Count had kept his promise and those I cared for were safe. Of course, that meant I truly had to keep my end of the deal now. I breathed a sigh of relief before coming to the next conclusion. The question escaped my lips before I had a chance to filter it.

"Did you order the attack on the village?" I knew that elite vampires like Vito could command armies, just as they were able to offer protection to younger vampires in exchange for servitude. We were taught in hunter academy that vampires only achieved elite status by having been a vampire for at least 200 years, and elite vampires were most often the ones in charge of armies. There weren't a great number of them, though, due to hunters. The questions began racing through my mind. *Did he order the attack on Dustin's old village in order to make him leave? Just how old is he? How old was he when he became a vampire? And how many vampires does he command?*

"Slow down, my dear hunter. I will answer your questions, but first," he stared into my eyes. *~Calm your mind.~*

I had dropped my defenses when I heard about Dustin and his family being safe, or perhaps Vito was able to break through easier because of my being close to him for an extended period of time, and my mind began to race through the questions immediately, which meant he heard them, and I was susceptible to his powers again. I vaguely realized this as my mind let go of my thoughts of its own accord.

"Now, I did not order the attack, although I had prior knowledge of it. As such, I knew I would be able to lay my claim on you tonight. I am 296 years old. I was born in 1714, and turned when I was 28 years old. I command vampires in three cities, and have around 20 servants here at the castle. Now, no more questions. It's time for dinner."

"Dinner?" I asked, incredulously. "Do vampires even eat?"

"We can, although we gain nothing from it. I didn't think you'd like to dine alone, however, and I don't believe you've eaten yet tonight?"

He was right that I hadn't eaten dinner. I had been distracted by his call and had decided to skip eating altogether because my stomach had been in knots. It was still twisted, but I figured I should eat something to keep my strength up, in case I needed to plot an escape.

I had also eaten alone enough years to know just how much I hated to be alone. Now the question looming before me was: is it better to eat alone or with a vampire? I hesitantly took the arm he offered me, my mind still reeling from my questions and his answers, and let him lead me to the dining hall, where the table was laden with a variety of foods.

"Wine?" he offered.

"Water." I had only tried wine once or twice, at hunter parties celebrating the takedown of hordes of vampires. One I had tried tasted ok, but I didn't like how it made my head feel sort of foggy and jumbled.

I couldn't afford to let any wine cloud my judgement tonight. I was already having a difficult time getting my defenses back in place, and the wine would only serve to slow my thinking down even more. Vito ordered a servant to my side, who prepared my plate with anything I asked for. The food smelled delicious, and as much as I hated to admit it, I thoroughly enjoyed the dinner. It was far beyond the cooking skills of myself or Dustin.

I ate slowly, cutting my steak into small, bite-sized pieces, trying to buy myself some time. Vito, however, didn't seem to mind. He ate a few bites to be polite, but mostly sipped from his wine goblet that was filled with a thick red liquid I could only assume was blood. I shuddered at the thought.

As I finished my last bite and dabbed my face clean, he stood and came to my side. Taking my hand, he helped me stand and led me from the dining hall. Part of me was grateful for his help, as I wobbled a bit in the heels he had laid out to go with the dress for tonight. I wasn't used to wearing heels, so I wasn't too surprised that I was a bit wobbly in them.

"What now?" I cautiously asked as he slowly led me back up the grand staircase and back to my chambers.

"Now, my sweet hunter," he paused as we reached my door and kissed my hand. "You sleep."

"I sleep?" He was kidding, right? What was the point of bringing me here just to feed me dinner and let me sleep? This made absolutely no sense.

"Yes," he said with a smirk. "You must be tired. I don't plan to turn you yet, my dear. Unless, of course, you wanted me to?"

He chuckled as I shrank back from him ever so slightly. I couldn't go too far, as he still held my hand gently but firmly in his own.

"You can sleep peacefully." He pulled me toward him and placed a kiss on my shoulder before walking away. I stood there for a moment, watching as he walked further and further away from me, my mind in a complete jumble. None of this evening made any sense.

I entered my room and found pajamas in the closet. I changed and grabbed my old teddy bear before crawling into the large bed. *Why didn't he change me? What is he planning? What would my parents think if they were here right now?*

The last one was easy to answer. My parents would storm through the doors of the castle and demand my return, killing any vampires who got in their way. I hugged my teddy bear closer, the thought of my parents bringing tears to my eyes as I began to drift off to sleep. Had I let them down? I tried to fight sleep as a familiar sense washed over me. It was a sense of being watched. The ever close proximity of Vito loomed over me as I noticed a shadow sitting in the corner before I couldn't fight the sleep any longer.

Chapter 5

The next morning I woke up with a start, and bolted into a sitting position. It took a moment for the memories of last night to hit me, and even then they were a bit blurry. Dustin's village. The deal with Vito. The castle. The room. Dinner. The kiss on my hand, and then the one on my shoulder. Sleep. My hands reached to feel both sides of my neck. He hadn't turned me. Why? I looked at the room around me, my eyes stopping at the figure sitting in the chair in the corner of my room, gently closing a book and setting it on the table next to the chair.

"Good morning, my dear hunter. I trust you slept well?"

"I feel like I was drugged, actually." I slowly dropped my hands to my lap.

"A nice perception you have there. Only a mild sedative, I assure you."

"Why?"

"I couldn't have you trying to escape on your first night here, now could I? Not with what I have in store for you today."

I raised an eyebrow at him. So, he granted me a final day as human? Was that it? There came a knock on the door and Vito gave permission to enter the room, never minding the fact that I was sitting in bed, in pajamas. What did modesty matter to a vampire, right? Another vampire entered carrying a tray with a plate of food and a red rose on it. Vito took it from him and brought it to me.

"Another sedative?" I could hardly trust him or the food he provided now.

"A birthday breakfast. You are officially an adult now, my dear."

It hit me like a ton of bricks. I didn't really celebrate my birthday much since losing my parents, so I didn't really keep track of the days surrounding what was supposed to be a special day for me. Who would I have wanted to celebrate with? But today was my eighteenth birthday already.

And that was when it dawned on me: once a vampire has control of their impulses, they avoid turning anyone who is not considered an adult. Of course, the age of adulthood changed over the centuries, but the idea was that vampires who had been turned at a younger age were more difficult when it came to teaching them how to control their impulses. Not like a day made a huge difference, but now I was considered an adult and fair game.

He watched me intently as I came to this realization and pushed the food tray away from me. "I'm not hungry."

"Eat, my dear. You will need your energy for today."

"And why's that?"

"We are hosting a party tonight, where you are the guest of honor. I shall present you to the vampires whom live in this area, whence they shall know that you're claimed. Mine."

I shuddered at the thought, and could only imagine that meant he'd be turning me at some point today, probably after this grand party he had planned.

I looked away from him, away from the food, and stared out of the large window. The beautiful hills and mountains seemed a little fuzzy against the mostly cloudy sky outside. It's odd how we notice the weather most often when it reflects how we're feeling.

~*Eat.*~ His voice commanded inside my head again. I slowly picked up the fork and began taking small bites of food. I needed him out so that I could think. Maybe eating would accomplish that.

"And just how long is this *game* of yours going to last?" I asked between bites.

"I'm not sure. I do enjoy playing with you, *hunter*," he spoke the words with amusement evident in his voice and ran his fingers through my hair, allowing it to drop slowly back down onto my shoulder, before leaning in and adding, "or perhaps I should start calling you Countess now, so you get used to it?"

"I'm still a hunter," I spat. "My goal is to protect innocent people from the likes of *you*, which is exactly what I did by agreeing to come here with you."

"Yes, *you* were the one who agreed to join me here, and you'd do well to remember it, my dear." He turned and took a few steps toward my bedroom door before calling back at me, "peruse your closet. There are suitable gowns for tonight. My servants are here to tend to any need you may have."

I watched as he walked out the door. Was this my new life? Had I become a play toy for this vampire in order to save my partner and his family? Moments after he left my room, another vampire came in. This time, it was a female vampire. She said her name was Gabrielle, offered to take care of anything I needed, and inquired as to what I'd like to wear for the day and what gown for this evening. Like I actually cared. However, she seemed nice enough, so maybe it wouldn't be too bad having someone to talk to other than my own private warden.

I spent the morning perusing the vast library, which was full of various books about vampire history and lore, with some obviously antique books on the shelves too high for me to reach. Might not be a bad idea to learn some new things, at least. Maybe even weaknesses I could pass along to Dustin somehow. Unfortunately, it seemed that these books didn't contain much information beyond what I had already learned from the academy or in daily life fighting against vampires.

I saw a slew of vampires rushing here and there, preparing for the grand party the Count was holding in my honor. The only problem with the party was that I couldn't find a way to ditch it. The castle was locked up tight, and with the servant Vito assigned to me tagging along wherever I went, I was almost never alone. I at least had privacy in the bathroom, but only barely due to vampires having a supersonic sense of hearing.

The worst part of it all was that part of me didn't want to run away. I kept berating that part, but it wouldn't budge. I wanted to hate Vito with all of my being, but that one part of me kept telling me I couldn't hate him. Not entirely. He had, after all, protected me for many years. I sighed as I made my way back to my quarters and into my closet.

The hours had passed quickly while I was looking through the books in the library, probably due to the dread I felt for tonight. Might as well decide what to wear tonight.

I settled on a black dress with spaghetti straps that came to just above my knees, with a black sheer material that opened in front and came down to my ankles. I didn't think wearing red was a good idea in a castle full of vampires, and black seemed like a fitting color for celebrating the end of my life as I knew it.

I dressed myself and allowed Gabrielle to fix my hair, which she curled and pinned into a fancy up do. I shuddered at least a few times simply from the knowledge that there was a vampire right behind me, and there was nothing I could do about it right now. I slipped on a pair of black open toe heels with rhinestones all over them and gazed at myself in the mirror. This was the second time seeing myself in this mirror dressed nicely. It was just as hard this time to admit that it was me in the mirror as it had been the day before.

This is it, I thought to myself as I heard a rapping at my chamber doors. Gabrielle waited for my nod and then opened the door, allowing the Count to enter. He had also dressed for the occasion, donning an emerald green button down shirt tonight, wearing a three piece black suit along with it. For some reason, it looked elegant on him, rather than overkill.

"We must prepare to greet our guests, my dear," he said as he offered his hand. With a steadying breath, I stepped next to him, but left his hand waiting, which didn't seem to faze him. He instead placed the waiting hand on the small of my back, as if to guide me along. "Let us go downstairs to the ballroom, and I will show you what to expect for tonight."

Before I could respond, there was a loud crash and the sound of gunfire. Vito left my side quickly, telling me to stay put. Another loud crashing sound.

"Knock, knock!"

I ran from my room. "Dustin?? Is that you?"

"Damn Skippy!"

Vito was standing at the top of the stairs. He looked at me and I saw fire in his eyes. "You stay here, and stay quiet."

"Fat chance," I muttered.

As Vito jumped down to the first floor, I took quickly to the steps. It only took a couple of steps for me to stop and take the shoes off. Heels weren't really good shoes for running in, and much less for fighting in. Dustin met me at the base of the stairs, firing a couple of shots in Vito's direction.

"What are you doing here?!"

"I got your note. You could've left me an easier clue, you know. 'Made deal with vamp to save your village.' I can't believe you made a deal with *this* Count!" Another few shots, which Vito easily dodged.

"You will not leave here alive, hunter." I looked into his eyes, burning with rage, and couldn't tell if he meant Dustin would die, or if he meant he'd turn me into a vampire before we could escape.

"We'll see about that, Vamps." Dustin reloaded his gun and took a few more shots, backing me towards the entrance of the castle.

Vito removed two rapiers from the wall. "Why don't you put your toy away and fight me proper, man to man?"

"Have it your way." Dustin bolstered his gun and Vito slid one of the swords across the floor to him. "Kel, run! Go get to safety."

I could see a few other hunters just outside the opening to the castle. Dustin had brought a group with him in his attempt to save me. "No, I'm a hunter, too. I'll stay and fight."

"Kel, go! This is between me and him. For attacking my family."

~You should listen to him, my dear. Go back to your chambers.~

"I'm not going anywhere." My answer was directed at the both of them.

Dustin pushed me aside, into a chair, as Vito took his stance to begin their swordplay. A quick lunge towards Dustin, who parried the attack with a soft clang of the swords.

"Good show, hunter. Perhaps you have a back bone after all."

I moved to get up from the chair, when Vito's voice filled my mind again.

~You stay put, dearest.~ Vito had penetrated through my defenses entirely now, and I sat, paralyzed, as I watched the two lunge at each other again, swords clanging over and over again. It

seemed I was right. The longer I was here, close to the Count, the easier it was for him to enter my mind. Now I not only heard him speaking in my mind, but he also had some control over my ability to move.

"Bring it," Dustin replied as he advanced on the Count, who took a step back and with a slight flick of his wrist cut Dustin in the arm.

Dustin winced at the cut, and muttered "luck," before lunging at the Count once again. Vito was ready, however, and executed a parry that forced Dustin's arm up with the sword, followed by a swift sweep of the leg, kicking Dustin's legs out from under him. Rolling into a recovery, he lunged back at the Count. I watched as Dustin tried over and over to make a mark on the Count, but Vito seemed always one small step ahead, and so Dustin's sword never made contact with him.

This continued for what felt like forever as I sat, unable to move from the chair, watching as the swords made contact over and over again, until finally I managed to put my defenses in place once again, just as Vito's sword made contact with Dustin's abdomen. I leapt from the chair to Dustin's side, causing Vito to abandon his next attack.

I pulled Dustin away as much as I could before some of the other hunters from the group finally burst in and assessed the situation. Taking Dustin from me, they pulled him quickly from the castle, as he muttered "this isn't over."

"I'll be waiting, hunter," Vito spat as I followed the other hunters out. They hurried Dustin to the nearest village and called for the doctor as Dustin grit his teeth in pain.

"He's having trouble breathing," I said as we hurried to the village clinic. Why did vampires always have to live so far from the big cities where they had the best doctors? I knew, of course, that it made it easier for them to hide away undetected, but in that moment I cursed it anyway. I held Dustin's hand as the others laid him on the floor in the clinic to wait for the doctor.

"Kel," he whispered as he looked at me before slipping unconscious.

"Dustin, no. Wake up. Don't do this to me," I softly caressed his face. The doctor had two attendants with him, whom he ordered to place Dustin on a stretcher and they took him to a back room. Waiting for news with the other hunters felt like hours. Finally, the doctor came back out.

"He'll be ok. I stitched up his wound and I've started him on a blood transfusion. His consent was already on file, thankfully. But he possibly has two broken ribs, and one might be pushing up against his lungs. His lungs don't seem punctured, but I've called an ambulance to transport him to the city hospital, just in case. He'll need x-rays and to stay there for observation for a day or two. He'll also need a lot of rest, and is unable to hunt for two to four weeks. Is there anyone at home who is able to help take care of him?"

Sometimes, these village doctors could surprise you. We had all kinds of consent forms on file with local villages all around, in case something like this should happen. I guess these doctors saw enough patients to know which injuries happened during hunts.

"I can," I stood up. Dustin took care of me when I was injured. He was my partner, so of course I'd be the one to take care of him. That was another big part of the reason for having a partner. I spent the next day getting food and supplies so I'd be ready for him to come home, even setting up the guestroom downstairs for him.

The time alone gave me plenty of time to think about all that had happened. What a way to spend my 18th birthday. I had felt like I had no option other than to go with Vito. And Vito… he could have easily captured me while I struggled to pull Dustin away. Why did he let us go? There were so many things about that experience that just didn't seem to fit together, no matter how I tried.

Finally, Dustin was able to come home, which meant it was now my turn to annoy him with caregiving, just like he had done for me. I knocked on his bedroom door the next morning.

"Everything ok in there?"

"I think so. C'mon in, I'm halfway dressed."

I walked in and sat in the chair I had set up next to the bed. I felt guilty he had been hurt. "How do you feel?" It must've been at least the tenth time I've asked since he came home the night before.

"Like crap, but that's ok. Everything in my body hurts. But hey, at least no punctured lungs."

"Dustin," I began, looking down at my hands as I wrung them in my lap. I wasn't exactly sure what I was going to say, but when the words formed on my lips, they began spilling from my mouth out of control. "I am so sorry. This was all my fault. I never should have made that deal with him, I should have just stayed home and waited for you, I should've-"

He grabbed my hand and set it on the bed in his. "It's ok. He was using mind control, and you did what you could to keep my family safe. That means more than you know."

I sighed. I couldn't bear to tell him the deal had been my idea. Of course, now that I had the chance to really think about it, I wondered if the idea had really been mine to begin with. "I know, I just... I feel like I could've done something more. Something different."

"You couldn't have. It's ok, Kel. Besides, it's only fractured ribs, not completely broken. You don't need to feel so bad. This is expected in our line of work." He grimaced as he took a deep breath.

I placed a hand on his shoulder. I wanted to hug him, but I knew if I tried it would only hurt him more. "Do you need anything?"

"Yes, actually. Some new ribs would be good. Or a nice, hot bath, but I don't think I'd be able to get in the bath right now."

"Oh, umm... I could wash you up if you want." I blushed. I hadn't thought about the fact that he might have a hard time washing when I said I'd take care of him, and I didn't look forward to that.

"No," he laughed. "I'm fine. Actually, I just want to sleep right now."

"Ok, you got it. Let me know if you need anything." I stood up and headed towards the door, happy to get out of there without having to actually give him a sponge bath. I wasn't sure how well I could handle something like that.

"Kel?"

"Yeah?" I turned my head back to see him smiling gently at me.

"Thank you."

I smiled back at him before making my way out of the room and down to the basement. I didn't want him to change his mind about getting washed up, and doing a bit of training would offer a good distraction from the thoughts that kept racing through my head.

Had it actually been my idea to go with Vito? Or was that one of his mind games? Had he been planning on changing me that night? And the fight with Dustin... Vito clearly had the upper hand in that fight. Dustin could've been killed. Vito's eyes were on fire when Dustin barged in. I thought for sure he was going to kill him.

Chapter 6

I opened my eyes as the first rays of light made their way through the bedroom window. It took me a moment to get my bearings: I had fallen asleep sitting on the floor of the guest room, leaning against Dustin's bed.

"Dustin? Are you awake?" I mumbled as I rubbed the sleep from my eyes and stood up to look down at him, soundly asleep in his bed. He looked like he was dreaming – a pleasant dream, judging by the slight smile. He looked like an angel, laying there peacefully and not fighting with me like he usually does.

I sat on the full sized bed next to him, leaning back against the headboard. I held my breath as he stirred before settling back into a peaceful sleep. I placed a gentle kiss on his nose before laying down next to him.

"Mmmm," he leaned his head against mine before adding a half-asleep "good morning."

"Good morning, Sleeping Beauty," I smiled.

He squeezed his eyes tightly closed. "'Good morning, Sleeping Beauty?' Was I talking in my sleep or something again?"

"You said a couple things, but I couldn't understand what they were." I placed a small kiss on his forehead as he smiled.

"Hmm. That might be for the best then." He stole a quick, sleepy glance at me.

"Oh? And just what do you think you said?"

"I have no idea," he said with a small shrug. "Just going by what I was dreaming about."

"And that was…?"

"Just pleasant dreams for a change." He had a sheepish grin on his face.

"Well, if it was a good dream, does that mean you're feeling better today?"

"I'm feeling much better now."

"Good. I'm glad you're ok, Dustin."

"And I'm glad you're ok." He stared at me now. "You had me worried sick, Kel. And jealous," he muttered under his breath.

Did I catch that right? Did he say he was jealous? What reason could he have possibly had to be jealous? "Why were you jealous?"

"Well," he hedged, "you went off with the vampire we've been hunting. Why do you think I'd be jealous?"

"Well, maybe because I was about to become a vampire countess? And possibly willingly?" I stared at him with my eyebrows raised, halfway joking with him and halfway unsure of what to think.

"Kel… I'm just glad you're back. I-" he caught his breath, as if he were unsure that he wanted to continue. "I love you. A lot."

I propped myself up on my elbows and looked down at him. He looked ready for a verbal assault. A rejection. "I love you, too, Dustin." The words surprised me easily as much as they surprised him.

"Kel…" He seemed unsure of what to say next. Whatever he was expecting, it hadn't been for me to reciprocate his feelings. "I still can't believe you made that deal. What were you thinking?"

"I just… when Vito showed up here after you left, I knew I had to do something. He promised the safety of both you and your family. You know he's an elite vampire. He has the power to do that."

"So he called for the attack to lure you into that trap?"

"No. I asked. He knew about it, though. But while I was there, I kept thinking about his plans for me and what my parents would think… I tried everything I could to not think of you. If he broke through my defenses and heard me thinking about you-" I paused and shuddered. "I just can't imagine what he would do."

He looked at me, his face a mixture of shock and… guilt?

"Kel… I'm sorry."

"What are you sorry for?"

"I'm sorry that you had to bargain your life for me and my family. I've never wanted you to do that. It's not fair to you."

"I… it didn't… I mean," I stammered and then sighed. "Dustin, I love you, and I will do anything to make sure you're ok. I just didn't realize I loved you until recently." *I may not have figured it out if Vito hadn't pointed out that Dustin loves me. But wait… why did he? He's claimed to have feelings for me for so long, so why add Dustin to the mix? What is he planning?*

"What are you thinking right now?" Dustin's words snapped me out of my daze and I shook my head.

"Hm? Oh, nothing, really. Just that…" Food. That's a good excuse. I always seem distracted when I'm hungry anyway. "I'm hungry. What do you want for breakfast?" I watched his face as nonchalantly as I could, and saw it change slightly. It reminded me of when I used to practice putting up my defenses and would watch myself in the mirror. The tiny changes that told me my mental defenses were up. Was he putting up defenses, too?

"Umm, not sure. What do we have?"

"Well, I could make pancakes, waffles, French toast, eggs sunny-side up or scrambled, bacon, sausage… or I could just get you an old-fashioned bowl of cereal." I laughed nervously. I was glad for the change of direction in our conversation. I wasn't good at letting people get close to me, and I was even worse at admitting when I wanted someone to be close to me. Not a surprise, of course, given my history.

"Uh, ok. Whatever is easier? Probably the cereal, it doesn't need much work."

I rolled my eyes. Did I have to remind him that between the two of us, I was definitely the better cook, so easy or difficult wasn't a concern? "It doesn't matter what's easiest, what do you *want*?"

"Ok, ok… I guess waffles."

"Waffles it is." I got up and walked out the door before he could respond. In the kitchen, I reveled in my solitude and allowed my thoughts to wander while I cooked. That was actually my favorite part of cooking.

Why does he do that? Is he trying to be a pain? Did I do this to him when he had to take care of me? Hmmm... probably. I shouldn't get too annoyed with him; neither of us handle being injured very well. And it's not like I can blame him – he came to rescue me, after all.

That stopped me dead in my tracks. Dustin had come to save me. Save me from Vito. *Vito wasn't injured. Dustin never landed a single strike. And Vito held back. I've seen him against other hunters before, and his strikes were never delicate. He let us go. Why did he allow us to escape? He could've killed Dustin right then. Of course, then our contract would be null and void. I guess it already was, since he injured Dustin. Maybe that's why he let me escape.*

I thought back to Vito's face right before I followed my fellow hunters out of the castle. What was it I saw there? Definitely anger. But also… was it sadness? Betrayal? I looked down at the waffles I had made and noticed I had poured too much syrup on them while lost in my thoughts. I shook my head clear and carried the plateful of waffles and a glass of orange juice in to Dustin.

"Here you go, with lots of syrup, just like you like." His eyes widened as I placed the plate on his nightstand. Whatever his thoughts, he decided against saying anything about the waffles that were drowning in syrup. I'd say that was probably a smart move right now. Instead, he sat up and winced in pain. I grabbed a back cushion and placed it behind him.

"You ok? I mean, you don't need me to feed you or anything, right?" I raised an eyebrow and smirked. Back to our old jokes and jabs. Comfortable conversation material.

"I'm not that helpless, am I?" he chuckled.

"I don't know, *are* you?" I laughed. His response was to stab the drowning waffle with his fork and take a bite.

"Wow, this is good," he said around the mouthful of waffle. Swallowing, he offered me a bite.

"No, that's ok. I'm good."

"Are you trying to say that these are poisoned?" He raised an eyebrow at me and I laughed. My first real laugh in days. It felt both comfortable and strange.

"No, I'm just saying you eat them. You're going to need your strength for healing, right?" I smirked at him. It was nice to be able to throw his own words back at him.

* * * * *

The next two weeks passed by somewhat uneventful, thankfully. No vampire attacks, and no mention of the Count. I did go on a few hunts with a local group of hunters. Mostly just low level vampires of very little skill. Probably recently changed, so they hadn't had a chance to hone their undead abilities yet, which was good. It also meant they hadn't had a chance to turn a lot of people yet, either. The earlier in the undead lives we could take them out, the better. It was nice to be out on hunts, getting back into the groove of things. It always felt weird not having Dustin to have my back, though.

Dustin was given clearance to train again, and so he was once again downstairs in the gym. I decided to go in and check on him, and found him standing in the padded area of the gym, practicing his hand to hand combat moves. I watched from the corner for a few minutes, admiring his smooth muscles as they flexed and contracted with his movements, and noticed a sword on the floor nearby. He must've been practicing his swordplay a bit as well. No doubt a result of his unfinished fight with Vito.

I had come to accept the fact that I did, indeed, love him. Along with that acceptance, I started noticing small things like the way the sun reflected in his hazel eyes, the way his muscles moved during training, or how he would mutter to himself while training. Today, I specifically noticed he seemed lost in thought, so I threw a ball at him.

"Your left side guard is down, Dustin," I called out. He startled as the ball raced past his face and turned toward me.

"Geeze, Kel, you scared the heck outta me!"

"Well, your left side guard was down. And you weren't paying attention to your surroundings. Always pay attention to your surroundings." He walked over to the vaulting horse and grabbed his towel, dabbing sweat from his face. *He's gorgeous like this.... ack, no, I'm doing it again. Clear your mind, Kel. Focus.*

"I suppose you're right."

"Of course I'm right. I was watching you. I notice things."

"I'll bet," he mumbled. "Well then, would you like to go a couple of rounds to teach me your flawless technique?"

"Nope. I got my training in the other night on the hunt. I was just coming down here to let you know lunch is in the oven. Can't train on an empty stomach, right?" There was no way I could spar with him while my mind was so distracted.

He raised his eyebrow at me. "Right. Well, that's ok. I understand if you don't want to go against me." He used a teasing tone. We both knew that despite my flexibility giving me the advantage many times, he was definitely the stronger one in hand to hand combat. "Lunch, however, does sound good right about now." He paused and wiped more sweat from his face. "So does a shower."

"Well, don't take too long. Pizza's already in the oven." I gave him a quick smile before heading upstairs. He followed along behind me, turning off the light in the basement. We had formed something that may pass for a relationship, at least among young hunters, even though we didn't really discuss our feelings too often. A peck on the cheek or a tight embrace. Sometimes just a smile that conveyed our emotions. Our trust. At least it was something.

I still held back, though. More recently, however, I wasn't sure if I held back because I was afraid of what Vito would do, or because of the guilt I felt every time I thought of the Count and his face as we fled the castle. I was actually concerned about the fact that Vito allowed our little displays of affection.

Being a teenager was turmoil. I thought I knew what I wanted. I loved Dustin and knew that now. But the guilt tore at me, too. Why couldn't I just have a relationship like a normal teenage girl? *Because I'm a vampire hunter, that's why. And normal teenage girls aren't vampire hunters. Then there's also Vito…*

We sat in the living room and ate the pizza while watching old reruns on the TV. It was easier than the silence when I didn't feel like talking, and Dustin knew not to push when I felt this way. The phone rang, and Dustin answered. He'd started answering more phone calls since the night Vito had called and informed me I would be his that night. This time, his face broke into a smile. I knew that look – we got a call for work. It was time to gear up and go hunting.

It was Dustin's first hunt since that night at the Count's castle, and I could tell he was excited to get back into action. I felt better knowing we'd have a group of fellow hunters around in case he wasn't feeling completely normal yet.

"Where's the target?"

"About twenty miles due south, just on the other side of the mountain. Seems there's a vampire down there with a horde, trying to make a name for himself. He's already killed a few locals, and turned a few others."

"Let's do this." I grinned and went downstairs for my gear. I grabbed my favorite silver dagger and a small pistol that I attached in a holster to my ankle. Dustin grabbed a couple of handguns and a sword. Evidently that swordfight with Vito was really sticking with him. He didn't usually grab a sword for our hunts.

We met up with the small hunter group at the base of the mountain and made our way towards the village where the vampire horde had been wreaking havoc. A high-pitched scream told us exactly where to find them, and we leapt into action without a second thought.

The ensuing melee lasted all of half an hour or so. This group of hunters was vigorous, for sure. The fight was full of flashes coming from handguns with specialized bullets and daggers gleaming in the moonlight. Most of the bodies that littered the ground were those of vampires, and our casualties were minimal. Towards the end of the fight, as I slashed through a vampire that was charging at me, I noticed one vampire fleeing in the distance.

The resulting bonfire was a decent sized one, and the locals all came out to celebrate. All in all, it was a good night. Dustin and I compared our numbers, and he teased me for getting one more than I did, then we both fell into our beds that night exhausted. A few days of rest were quite welcome, but also left me free to let my mind wander.

It's been a few weeks since I've heard anything from Vito. Should I be worried? Is he planning something?

"Kel?"

Why can't I get him out of my mind, even when he isn't talking to me? I just feel like there's something about that night that I'm missing.

"Kel!"

"Huh? What?" I snapped my head over to Dustin, who was sitting at the kitchen table reading some papers.

"I'm pretty sure the eggs are dead. You can stop beating them now."

"Oh, right," I felt my face flush as I poured the scrambled eggs into the frying pan.

"You ok? You seem a little dazed."

"Yeah. Yeah, I'm good."

"Mm-hmm."

"Really, I'm fine. Just tired. Haven't been sleeping well the last couple of nights."

"You'd think killing all those vamps the other night would help you sleep better."

"Yeah, you'd think so." But I couldn't get my mind off the one vampire that really mattered. The one I needed to kill.

"Well, don't forget we got another big hunt tonight."

"I'm looking forward to it," I smiled as I set our plates of scrambled eggs on the table. "Gotta keep up the practice." *Especially if I'm going to face Vito and defeat him one day. Hopefully soon. Then maybe I can stop beating myself up over all of this.*

"Speaking of... you wanna go downstairs after breakfast for some sparring?"

"Sure."

So after breakfast, we went downstairs for a light warmup and some sparring time. Dustin beat me almost every time, but it was nice to pin him a few times, too. Before we knew it, the time had come to prepare for the evening's hunt, and we had been promised it would be a good one.

Chapter 7

I looked over my shoulder from the sofa and could see Dustin in the kitchen, rinsing off his plate before loading it into the dishwasher and running the load. He looked tired, and for good reason. Last night's hunt was rough – one of the vampires had convinced a few werewolves to fight alongside him. Dustin rolled his shoulders back and stretched his neck as he walked to the desk in the living room and sat down at the computer.

"You alright, Dustin? Last night wasn't an easy fight… Thanks to you being so stubborn again."

"Me, stubborn?" He pointed to himself and raised his eyebrows incredulously, making me laugh.

"Yeah, you."

"How was I being stubborn?"

"Well, if you'd try doing things my way once in a while, you might not get so torn up when you fight. Brains over brawns?"

"Yeah, well you try doing that when you have a six foot something, two hundred plus pound beast running in your general direction. My first instinct was to charge it 'cause it was going after you when you were dealing with that vamp. So *excuse me* if I rushed in."

"And *that* is why I handle the vampires," I rolled my eyes at him. "The ones with brains."

He chuckled and rolled his eyes back at me as he turned toward the computer. "Whatever, Kel." A few clicks and he pulled up a website. My curiosity got the best of me and I walked up behind him.

"What're you looking at?" I looked over his shoulder.

"Well, I've heard of a few hunters putting up some stuff about vamps on the net, so I figured I'd check it out. It's somewhat easier than heading down to the Raven for info, though I plan to do that later, too."

"Ah… find anything yet?"

"A few things. Mostly stupid stuff that we already know about."

"Figures. They're always two steps behind."

"Exactly." I could hear him grinning. He took pride in being a top hunter in our age group. Heck, he was almost as good as some of the seasoned hunters ten years older than us. Part of that came from his network of resources. He was a pretty likable guy overall, so other hunters were always willing to divulge information to him. And he had a knack for getting bits of information from several other hunters and then piecing it all together like some sort of puzzle.

"Well, what did you expect? Are any of them pros like us?"

"One, evidently."

I gave him a sideways look. "Really? And what did they have to say about them?"

"They said something about a new hunting group in town. Hang on, let me pull up that page." He opened a new forum page and scrolled quickly. "Here we go. 'News spreads quickly around town of a new hunting group calling themselves the Night Hunters. This group is responsible for…' Wow. 'Cleaning out at least two towns and slaying Count Vito's younger brother. The leader of this group is a seasoned vampire hunter named Claudia Nemzeck.'"

I looked at Dustin when he paused. "Dustin? You alright? What's up?"

"Claudia Nemzeck," he whispered.

"Ok…? Dustin?"

He shook his head suddenly. "Huh? Yeah, yeah I'm ok."

"Who's Claudia Nemzeck?"

"Only a girl I used to know in the most unpleasant of ways."

"How so?"

He closed his eyes and shook his head. "Ancient history, Kel. Ancient history." He stood from the computer and started heading towards the stairs.

"Do tell, Dustin. We're partners. I should know a little about your history, especially if it's about a fellow vampire hunter."

He turned toward me and considered it for a moment. He must've decided I was right. With a sigh, he headed towards the sofa to sit. "Ok then. Take a seat."

I sat and waited for him to collect his thoughts. The look on his face told me this was no easy story for him to tell.

"Back when my brother and I were in the same hunting clan, we got a few new people one year. One of them was this girl. She was maybe a tad taller than you, with dark purple hair and eyes to match. A complete knockout. Anyway, that's not important. Over the months, we fought alongside each other and sooner or later we got emotionally involved. I didn't know what a mistake it was until it was too late. Soon after the year ended, she just got up and left with some other guy who promised her the world. I knew darn well he wouldn't give it to her, but he managed to convince her to believe his little fantasy tales. I tried to stop her, but she threw it back in my face by saying I didn't know what I was talking about and that I was just being jealous."

He sighed heavily. "She left me that night with a slap to the face. Last I heard she had been bitten by a vamp and became one of them. I guess I was wrong to believe third party information. Or maybe they were just trying to help me get over it."

"They who?"

"My other team members. Before we got split up."

"Oh. I'm sorry." I wasn't really sure what else to say. "I'm sure she doesn't realize what she's lost."

He shrugged. It was obviously still a painful memory for him, but he apparently didn't want to dwell on it. "Oh well. What's past is past. Yeah, it was a bad breakup. I hate her for it, just like she swore she hated me." He stood up then. "If you'll excuse me, sweetheart?"

I nodded, somewhat surprised. It was the first time he'd called me by any term of endearment since we said we loved each other. "Of course. Can I get you anything?"

He looked down and saw my eyes filled with tears. I couldn't help it. I knew next to nothing about Dustin's past, and it broke my heart that he'd been hurt like that.

"Yeah, maybe a bottle of water from the fridge. I'm gonna go get changed and find the punching bag downstairs."

I nodded as he made his way to his room upstairs. I went to the fridge and grabbed a couple of bottles of water for him. *He'll probably be down there for a bit. That is so sad. I had no idea.* I wiped the tears from my eyes as I heard Dustin walk down the stairs, but he noticed. Of course he did. We're hunters, trained to take in our surroundings at every moment.

"I'm sorry," he sighed.

"No, I'm sorry. I shouldn't have butt into your business." I could only imagine if he had asked me about any past boyfriends. How would I be able to explain that I'd only ever gotten close to one crush, and that Vito had made sure that it didn't go well? I fiddled with the ring on my necklace.

He shook his head. "No, it's ok. You were concerned and didn't know. I hadn't told you 'til now 'cause I thought she was dead. In my eyes, she's still dead, actually." He walked over to me and gave me a hug. Weird. I should be the one consoling him, not the other way around.

"You did nothing wrong. And it's not the end of the world. It's just a wound that I guess never fully healed." He looked down at me and gave a small smile, but I noticed his eyes were not their usual clear hazel, but a cloudy hazel. He may still view her as dead, but it obviously still hurt to think of her.

"Yeah, but still… I'm sorry it ever happened to you." I hugged him back and then pulled away to look him in the eyes. "You're a nice guy," I smirked and added "when you want to be."

He chuckled. "Trust me, back then I wasn't, so I guess I can't blame her too much."

"What, you? Not nice? Never!" I laughed. He hugged me close again and chuckled.

"Well, you still have your sarcasm so it looks like you'll be ok."

I hugged him back. "I guess so." Sarcasm wasn't just part of my personality. It was also one of my defense mechanisms. When I didn't know what to say, needed out of a situation, or just felt uncomfortable, sarcasm was my go-to. It was a lot easier than being honest with anyone, myself included. "To be honest," I sighed, "all I really wanna do is go pound in what's-her-name's face. Then I'd feel better."

He laughed. "You and me both. And I'd like to get my hands on that Daniel, or Jason, or whatever his name was. Maybe Ian? Oh well." He shrugged.

"Well, whoever he was, it sounds like she ditched him, too."

"Probably. But you know what?"

"Hmm?"

"I know something that might make you feel a whole lot better."

"What's that?" I didn't entirely trust the gleam in his eyes, and I was right not to. He took advantage of us standing so close and began to tickle my sides, causing me to squirm as I tried to escape. "Hey, no fair!"

"All's fair in love and war," he laughed.

"Hey now," I managed between giggles. "You're quoting my quotes."

"What do you expect? I live with you, don't I? I hear them all the time."

"True, but you know something?" I was struggling to breathe from the fit of giggles.

"What's that?" He stopped tickling me so I could talk for a moment. I struck quickly – a quick kiss on the lips and wriggled free.

"I still have the element of shock in my favor," I laughed and ran behind the sofa while he stood there with a mixed look of shock and amusement on his face. Until now, the only kisses we had shared were on the cheeks. He didn't know about the kiss I stole when he was asleep, the day Vito decided it was time to whisk me away and claim me. He knew how I felt about relationships. I had told him a little, but skirted around Vito being the main cause for my avoidance of intimacy with people.

"That you do," he grinned and began to chase me around the sofa. After a few rounds, he decided a direct attack would be more effective, and dove over the back of the sofa. I had moved just out of arm's reach though, and he face planted right into the cushions, legs flailing in the air.

I laughed as I stepped up to the sofa. "You alright down there?" A muffled groan. "Hello? Earth to Dustin?" I grabbed one of the bottles of water and poured a few drops onto his head. Unfortunately, I had to get a little too close to him to do so, and he grabbed my legs with one hand and used his other on my back to push me down to the sofa, spilling the water all over him. I let out a squeal as I fell to the sofa.

After his revenge attack, he sat up and shook his hands and head free of water. "Gee, thanks Kel. Now I'm all wet." He grabbed the bottle and dumped the remaining water on my head. "And now you are, too." He laughed again and I gaped at him, which gave him the chance to steal a kiss and wrap his arms around me.

"I love you, Dustin. I really do."

"I love you, too." It was only the second time we'd said those words since admitting our feelings. I wanted to tell him more. I wanted to tell him how those three little words meant so much more than I ever thought they could. That I'd never leave his side, no matter the dangers we'd face. But something was holding me back, making me feel on edge. Tense.

He pulled back and studied my face for a moment. He knew something was off, but there was no way he could know what. I didn't even know what was keeping me from saying more. "Are you ok?" I could see the concern in his eyes.

"Yeah," I nodded and looked around. The house needed tidying. It gave me a perfect excuse. How could I explain something I didn't understand myself? "Just thinking about the house. It's a mess, and it's my turn to clean."

"You're so random sometimes." He smiled at me. "Tell ya what. How about I go grab us a couple of towels, then give you a hand this time around? I'll tackle the kitchen, you do the living room. Whoever gets done first can double around and help the other."

"Yeah," I smiled. "That sounds good."

Once dried off, while he made his way to the kitchen, I started drying and fluffing the sofa cushions and found a couple of bouncy balls. I grinned and threw one in Dustin's direction, hitting him right in the back of the head.

"Owww," he groaned and turned to face me as I tried to stifle a giggle and rummaged through some papers, feigning innocence. "That's not funny."

"Yes, it is," I giggled. Bouncy balls were one way to relieve stress. It was childish, and we both knew it. But in our line of work, sometimes we needed to let our inner child out. He picked up the ball and shoved it into his pocket before going to the sink to wash the pans sitting there.

I stealthily made my way over to him and reached my hand into his pocket to retrieve the ball while his hands were busy washing pans, but his reactions were still quick, and he grabbed my arm with his soapy hand.

"Get your hand out of my pocket young lady. *Without* the ball in your hand." He didn't even bother to turn around and look at me.

"How can I take my hand out of your pocket if you're holding it in your pocket?"

"If I let go, will you take your hand out?"

"Yes, I will."

He removed his hand from my arm and tilted his head down. I knew he was watching to make sure I didn't try to steal the ball back. I removed my hand and took a few steps back toward the living room before removing the other ball from my own pocket and launching it at his head.

"The bouncy ball queen strikes again!" I laughed and ran up the stairs into my room. I saw him dry his hands quickly before chasing after me. I quickly darted into my bedroom and dove under my bed, placing a blanket over me. I calmed my breathing to slower, quiet breaths as I heard Dustin's footsteps in the hall, then in the bathroom.

"Where are you, Kel?" Next his bedroom. "Come out, come out, wherever you are." His footsteps quietly approached my bedroom. "Where could she be?" Rustling through the clothing in my closet.

"Ok, if I were Kel, where would I be?" He paused to think, then left my room. I shifted slightly before pausing myself. *Wait a second. This is Dustin, a fellow vampire hunter…*

I quietly crawled out from under my bed and tip toed to the door, then leapt across to the other side of the hallway. Judging by

Dustin's shocked look, he didn't expect me to suspect him being in the hallway, waiting for me.

"Eek, you really *were* there," I said in response to Dustin looking at me, arms crossed over his chest.

"Uh huh, and you were under the bed." I took off down the stairs, Dustin once again in chase. Into the kitchen, a couple of times around the table, and then I made my way to the sofa where I flopped down to catch my breath. Between running and laughing, I could barely breathe, but it was a nice feeling. Dustin sat on the edge of the sofa next to me.

"You, my lady, are difficult."

"Yes, yes I am."

"You're grounded. Go to bed." He laughed.

"Nope. Too tired to move. Nap, then we can go downstairs to train." I snuggled towards the back of the sofa on my side, freeing up space for him to sit comfortably. I felt him take a seat next to me and rest an arm on my arm. I felt tired, happy, and safe. It was a feeling that I knew wouldn't last long. It never did in a hunter's world. Before I knew it, I had fallen asleep.

Chapter 8

Another night, another fight. It felt like the battles with vampires never ended. Only this time, it was different. I hadn't had the chance to remove my necklace before going into battle. I usually only took it from my teddy bear's neck and put it on when I was really missing my parents. The chain held only my small gold ring with three hearts. And now? Now, a lousy vampire had torn it from my neck and the ring went flying.

In my fury, the next several minutes were a blur. The next thing I remembered was Count Vito wrapping his arms around me. I felt a blanket of warmth before looking back and seeing the offending vampire dead on the ground. My ring, however, was nowhere in sight. Everything went blurry as light began to hit my eyes.

I opened my eyes to find myself still laying on the sofa. I was alone. *Think*, I told myself. I fell asleep on the sofa last night, after the bouncy ball fight and chase with Dustin, then training. I looked down at my body and saw a warm blanket covering me. That had to have been the warmth I felt in my dream. Why did I associate it with Vito?

What else happened in that dream…? My ring! My hand raced to my neck. I had my necklace on yesterday, and I didn't remember taking it off. But when my hand reached my neck, there was nothing there. *Maybe I put it back on my bear?* I rose from the sofa and went to my room to check.

I heard the shower running as I passed by the bathroom and made my way into my room. My teddy bear was sitting on my bed, right where I left him. No necklace. No ring. I felt my heart start racing as I ran back downstairs to the living room. *Don't freak out, Kel. It probably just fell off in the sofa.*

Dustin came downstairs as I was tearing the cushions off of the sofa. I barely noticed him standing there as I searched frantically.

"Kel? What's wrong?"

"My necklace. It's gone."

He walked over to me as I kneeled in front of the sofa, fighting back the tears.

"The one with the ring on it?"

I nodded. "I woke up this morning, and it was missing. I know I had it on last night. I have no idea what could've happened to it."

"You checked your bear?"

"First place I checked. I thought maybe I had put it away and forgot. It's not there. I know I fell asleep with it on last night. It's not like it could've magically disappeared on its own." The tears started to fall as Dustin put his arms around me.

"We'll find it, Kel. Do you remember anything from last night?" He got on the floor to search under the sofa.

"Just a dream – hunting vampires. But…"

"But…?"

"In my dream, a vampire tore my necklace off. And then Vito was there. He killed the other vampire." I didn't dare tell Dustin that Vito held me close to him and I felt warm. Safe. "Oh, I did wake up once, but fell right back to sleep."

"What woke you up?"

"I don't know. I thought I heard something, but that's all I remember."

"Hmm."

"I can't remember anything else." He paused from his search to hug me.

"Shh. It's ok. We'll find it. It couldn't have just been magically swept away, and it's not like Vito came in and stole it."

"But… what if someone *did* take it?"

"How? I was next to you all night. I mean, don't get me wrong. We deal with some freaky stuff all day, but how could that happen without us waking up?" He got a strange look on his face. "You said you woke up in the middle of the night."

"Yeah, what of it?"

"Did you feel like something was askew when you woke up?"

"I don't know. It kinda felt chilly, but that was it."

"Not saying it's related or anything, but I woke up last night, getting a sort of invasion of privacy feeling. Like someone was looking over me while I slept, but it wasn't you. I always get a peaceful, soothing sort of feeling when you check on me during the night."

I felt my face flush. "You do?"

"Yeah. Call it a sixth sense I guess. I just know you're there, and it's calming. But last night, I felt really vulnerable and trapped. And… chilly. I almost never get chilly."

"I got chilly, too. You think it's a coincidence?"

"I don't know, but I'm starting to believe you were right." He put the sofa back together and sat down with a sigh.

"I was right about what? Someone taking it?" I sat next to him. *Vito was in my dream last night. Could he have taken it? It wouldn't be the first time he was here during the night.*

"Yeah. Not saying you are for sure, but it's getting convincing or I'm getting paranoid." He shrugged. "And don't even comment on that," he added with a smirk.

"Fine, no comment. But… how do we find my necklace now?"

He stood from the sofa and looked down at me. "There *is* this guy at the Raven. He's been saying stuff for a few days about people losing stuff out of thin air. Maybe we should try asking him a few questions?"

"Let me shower and change."

We had both been exhausted after a long and heavy training session last night, and fell asleep without showering. Now I felt gross from that and the potential invasion of privacy. Freshly washed, I felt a little more confident. I met Dustin downstairs in time to see him shove a knife into his combat boot.

"I thought The Raven didn't allow weapons?"

"Jimmy's working today. He'll let me in with it," he said with a wink. "You wanna drive?"

"No," I shook my head. "I'm too upset."

"Ok," he grinned and headed out to the car. I hopped into the passenger seat and put my dance music remix CD into the CD player. I needed some jams.

"You're only safe until the driver puts his belt on. Then panic," Dustin said as he put his seatbelt on, squealing the tires as we left the house.

"I started panicking the day I met you," I replied with a smirk. It wasn't entirely true, and he knew that. In fact, the day we met changed both of our lives. We had both been part of separate hunting clans. The clans had teamed up on a hunt for an elite vampire. Safety in numbers, and all that. I only hunted with the clan out of convenience. I was young and hadn't made a name for myself yet. Most people in the clan had partners they teamed up with on smaller hunts. In bigger hunts like this, partners were expected to watch each other's backs.

Hunters who didn't already have a partner established would be partnered up at random on bigger hunts like this one. Both Dustin and I were considered difficult to partner up, so we were stuck together on the hunt. Turns out it was fate, or luck, or whatever. Maybe thanks to our sarcasm or our shared desire to be the best, we actually got along. After the hunt, we agreed to stay partners, and the rest, as they say, is history.

"Here we are." Dustin's words brought me out of my memories and back to the present. Memories were more pleasant right now as anxiety took over.

"What if nobody has any information?"

"I'm sure there's something. We'll find it. Maybe even the one who stole it," he reassured me. "Now, when we go in, I'm going to hit up the bar and see if anyone's heard or seen anything, maybe see if Benny has any info on new vamps in town. You'll go talk to Wally. He typically sits in the far left corner of the club."

"Wait, I gotta talk to this guy myself? I don't even know him. What do I say? 'Hi, I'm a vampire hunter and I need to talk to you about things mysteriously disappearing lately. You mind if I ask you some questions?'" The sarcasm in my voice was oozing.

"He'll talk to you. Just tell him you're Kel and you have to talk to him. He likes talking to the ladies, and I've already told him if he ever touches you I'd cut off his hands," he grinned. "He's scum, but you'll be fine," he added when I stared at him incredulously.

"I just…" I looked down to the ground. I hated having to say the words that came out next. "I just feel vulnerable right now. And that feeling scares me. I always found strength through that ring."

Dustin held my hand. "I'll stay with you, then, and be your strength. Don't worry. Let's go."

It was my first time actually going to a club of any sort. I wasn't sure what to expect, but as we stepped up to the door my eyes took in the dimly lit room with groups of people spread all around. I couldn't see much else before there was a tough looking guy who had to have been over six feet tall standing before us. I knew from Dustin's previous tales that this was a bouncer – the guy in charge of letting us in and making sure we had no weapons. Jimmy, Dustin had said earlier.

"Well, if it isn't Dustin Sheen. How's it going, my man?"

"Brian! Man, I haven't seen you in a while. When did you get back into town?"

Brian? That was a name I hadn't heard. I looked back and forth between him and Dustin.

"About a week ago," Brian laughed before seeing me at Dustin's side. "My, who do we have here, Dustin?"

"Hey now," Dustin laughed. "That's my girlfriend you're talking about. Show some manners." He looked over at me. "Kel, I would like you to meet Brian Spillner, Loser Extraordinaire."

I chuckled a little, still nervous. "Nice to meet you, Brian."

"It's my pleasure, little lady. And don't let Dustin fool you. I saved his scrawny neck many a time back with the team." He flashed a grin my way. I was a little surprised – I hadn't met him that night Dustin and I partnered up, so I didn't remember him being on the team.

"Yeah, yeah. So, you gonna let us in or not?"

"Yeah, those were the days," Brian continued to reminisce. "We bagged vamps left and right, till that witch came along and broke up the team. What was her name again? Claudia something."

"Yeah, it was good times," Dustin responded, sounding tense. "It was Claudia Nemzeck, but let's not go there."

"Yeah, sorry bro. Not fond memories for us, especially Dustin," he spoke to me in a sorrowful voice. "Sorry for holding you up. You can head on in, just gotta check for weapons, first."

Dustin pulled something from his pocket. "Jimmy said to show any bouncer this card if they asked for my weapons."

Brian took a quick look before giving a curt nod. What was on that card Dustin showed? I tried to catch a glimpse before he shoved it back in his pocket, but couldn't make anything out. "No prob, Dustin. And I guess your lady friend is ok, too," he said as he stepped aside to let us in. "Nice to meet you, Kel," he called as we walked past.

I gave a quick nod and wave as the sounds of the club took over my senses. The music had a strong bass to it, and most of the club was dimly lit. There was an area set up for dancing, with strobe lights flashing over the people. Dustin grabbed hold of my hand, most likely sensing my overwhelm. My hunter senses were trying to take in every single detail. To be acutely aware of my surroundings. The problem was that there was too much to try to take in all at once. He pointed to the corner of the club. "That's Wally over there, the heavyset guy." He led me to the bar. "Want a drink? No drinking age, so you can have whatever."

I gave it some thought. Something to calm my nerves would be great, but I needed to keep my mind sharp. It was hard enough already, being nervous about what we'd find out.

~Go ahead, hunter. You deserve to relax and enjoy life at times.~

I stopped dead in my tracks. Having some warning when Vito would be entering my thoughts uninvited would have been nice, but he wasn't a knock first kind of guy in those situations. The last couple of weeks of quiet made his intrusion even more noticeable. Dustin cocked an eye at me, asking with his eyes what was wrong.

"I'll just take a water. Wanna stay sharp." *What do you want?*

~You'll find out soon enough, my dear.~

More of your mind games?

~Perhaps.~

Dustin walked up to the bar with me in tow. "Hey Benny. What's going on, man?"

"Business as usual. What can I get you two to drink tonight?" He nodded in my direction. Between him and the card thing with Brian, I got the feeling that Dustin came here a lot over the years, and was usually by himself.

"She'll take a water, I'll take my usual." I saw him whisper something else to Benny, but the music was too loud for me to make out what it was.

"Sure thing," Benny said as he dipped below the counter for a couple of glasses. Flourishing the glasses and putting on a show with the ice, he prepared my water and some sort of alcoholic beverage for Dustin. I didn't bother asking what it was. I had other things occupying my mind that kept me from enjoying his flashiness. Like Vito, and what his newest game might be.

"Thanks, Benny." Dustin handed me a water and a small glass of clear liquid that I suspected wasn't water. "Drink this. It'll help with your nerves." He turned back to Benny. "How much?"

"Well, if this is the girl that you're always talkin' about, then it's free. If not, then you've got some serious explaining to do. And fifty bucks to keep my mouth shut."

I looked at Dustin and raised an eyebrow. He talked about me? First Wally, and now Benny. Just how much did the people here know about me? Dustin just laughed.

"Yeah, this is her. And even if it wasn't, I got your fifty right here," he winked as he held up a fist. "Anyway, anything new going on around here?"

"Nah, the usual, other than Claudia being in town. She stopped by last night asking about you. I told her where you were living now. I figured it'd be a nice surprise for you to see her. Sounded like she wanted to patch thing up."

I could've sworn Dustin's jaw hit the counter. I didn't really know much about Claudia yet, but I knew from his reaction, this wasn't good. There had to be something more than just a bad breakup. I decided now was a good time to try that drink he got for me.

Chapter 9

"That's the problem with you, Benny. You think too friggin' much. What'd she say when you gave her the directions?"

"Actually, she sounded surprised that you're still alive. Said something about her new boy toy wanting to see you, too. Somethin' about an old sword match to finish. I just laughed and said that sounds like you to pick on someone bigger and older than you," Benny said with a shrug.

"Benny, you're like two seconds from getting a fist to the face. Was the guy with her?"

"Woah, chill big guy. Yeah, he was standing a ways back. Tall guy with I think dirty blonde hair. Hard to tell in this lighting. Anyway, he was dressed like he ran a country or some royal guy. Figures she'd go after the rich guys."

"Benny, if you weren't family, I'd kill you right now. You're just lucky you're my aunt's son, or you'd be on the floor already."

I grabbed Dustin's hand, which was tightly balled into a fist by his side. "Save it for Claudia," I whispered.

"Look, I'm sorry dude. I thought you might want to see her. She sounded real sincere when she asked. I know things didn't go well between you two, so I figured this might help. As for the guy? Well, it sounded like a joke when he laughed about it and called her a silly girl."

"Yeah, that sounds like him. A real character." Dustin took a big sip of his drink before slamming it down on the counter. "Later, Benny. I gotta go talk to Wally now."

"Yeah, alright man. I'll tell Mom you said hey."

I took a big gulp of water before setting my glass on the bar and waving goodbye to Benny. He saluted with two fingers from his forehead as Dustin started dragging me away.

"Dustin? I know this is strange and all, but you're starting to worry me. Me! I don't get worried because of peoples' actions. I know I don't know much about Claudia, but she sounds like bad news. And the guy she was with…" I didn't finish my sentence. I couldn't bring myself to even try. *Is this part of Vito's newest game?*

"Yeah, she's with Vito. Benny mentioned a sword fight that needs to be finished, and we didn't get to finish our fight when I rushed his castle to get you out of there. That was a dead giveaway."

"That and the 'silly girl' description. Not many people talk like that anymore."

"I'm sorry, Kel. It's bad enough she's in town, but starting to put the pieces together," he closed his eyes and stopped walking, letting out a heavy sigh. "Two of the people I would like to kill the most, and they're working together."

"Which is why it's good we're working together." I gave his hand a squeeze. "We make an amazing team. We can handle whatever they throw at us." *I hope so, at least. I know nothing about Claudia, but she sounds absolutely delightful.* Even my thoughts were dripping in sarcasm now.

~She may not be delightful, my dear. But she's efficient.~

Go away. I don't want to deal with you or your games right now.

Silence. Well, inside my mind, at least. The club was still blaringly loud. We were getting close to the dance floor now, with people shoving past us to go dance or take a break and go get drinks.

"Yeah, you're right." Another sigh. "Let's go talk to Wally. I'm pretty sure we won't get anything out of him that I haven't already figured out, though." He started walking towards the corner again, half dragging me along. Even in the dim light, I could see the scowl on his face. He wove us through the dance floor, with me almost running into people as I tried to keep up without jogging. He stopped in front of a table with a middle aged, balding man sitting with a girl in his arms and an armed thug standing behind him. Reminded me of those old mafia movies.

"Why hello there, Wally. That girl you have in your arms wouldn't be underage now, would she?"

"Well, if it isn't Mr. My-Daddy's-A-Sherriff-Goody-Two-Shoes himself, Dustin Sheen." Wally allowed his face to be overtaken by what seemed to be halfway a grin and halfway a sneer. The overall effect was rather disturbing.

"Why don't you have Vinny over there take Little Missy for a drive while we talk?"

A moment of hesitation, then he snapped his fingers and the bodyguard took the girl out the back door of the club. "So, Mr. Sheen, what can I do for you? Please, have a seat. Let's talk."

Dustin pulled a chair out for me and then took another chair himself. I sat quietly. I had never seen Dustin this angry and ready to blow. My normally confident and sarcastic self took a backseat for the caution I felt was needed now.

"We're here to ask you a few things about some missing property. Not you personally this time, but I thought you might know something about it."

"Let me guess," Wally replied with a sneer. "The girl here is missing a piece of jewelry, most likely a ring? Or a necklace? And you know I don't have it but you think I know who does. Am I right?"

Dustin glared at him. "Yeah, warlock, that's about right. So, what d'ya got for me?"

"Well," he started slowly, looking at me instead of Dustin. "I know you're missing a necklace. Probably something a dear family member gave you. As for who? I can find out, but it'll cost you."

I didn't like this man. Warlock or not, the way he leered at me gave me the creeps, and he wasn't being helpful in the least. "Where's my necklace?" I managed to say between my gritted teeth.

"Oh, I surprise you with my knowledge, huh? Well, let me tell you something, *Kel*. I know more and have greater powers than you think." He sat there looking smug and absolutely full of himself.

That's when it hit me. *He knows more than I think. He already knows who took my necklace. Probably in on the whole thing.* "Tell me where my necklace is. I know that you know."

"Look, Wally," Dustin slammed his fist on the table, getting Wally's attention again. "I'm not in the mood for your circus games. I know you're a middle-rate warlock, and I know you can read the minds of the untrained. And you've got your hands in just about everybody's business. Name your price and give us the information."

"Oh yes, for payment…" he looked over at me again. *Creepy,* I thought. *There's no way I'd do anything like that with him. Eww.*

"Don't even think about it," Dustin replied, daggers shooting from his eyes. Wally got a distant look in his eyes for a brief moment. "Cut to the chase, warlock. I'm growing impatient. You know that if you touch her, you die." *If you touch her, you die,* I repeated mentally. Normally Dustin would've said he'd kill him. Why did his phrasing put me off?

"Fine," Wally replied with a bite in his voice. "I'll tell ya. As for payment, Dustin, you can make it up to me later."

"Agreed," he sighed. "Now can we get some answers?"

"Yes. Follow me." Wally got up and began walking to the back room, which was hidden by a curtain. Dustin and I got up and followed quickly. The door had been locked, which gave us time to catch up to him.

"Stay on your guard," Dustin whispered to me as we got closer to Wally. "I don't like this one bit." I simply nodded as I heard the lock click and Wally opened the door into a dark room. My brain felt like it was floating around in my skull. I briefly wondered what that drink was that Dustin had given me before I entered the room behind Wally.

"Well, you wanted to know who has your necklace, right?" He flipped on the light switch. "Why don't you just ask her?"

I quickly took in the appearance of another young woman, sitting in a cushioned chair. She had dark purple hair that was wavy and fell to her low back, and she donned a dress that was the color of red wine, made of velvet. I silently thanked my hunter training for making this a natural reaction, because I had a feeling I'd have to hunt this woman down one day.

"You're Claudia, I presume?"

"Why yes, I am darling. And just who might you be?" She raised an eyebrow at me, and her whole aura screamed evil.

"You already know who I am, don't you?" I didn't wait for a response. "I'm Kel, and I believe you have something of mine. Return it."

She touched a gold chain that hung from her neck and gave a fake look of innocence. "Aww, is this yours?" She uncrossed her legs and stood from the chair, taking a single step forward, pulling my ring out from under her dress. As she stood, I could tell she was about five foot six or so, and was built rather thin.

"Give it back, Claudia. Now! Whatever your deal is, she has nothing to do with it." Dustin stepped forward, his fists balled up and ready to let loose.

"Temper, temper, darling. I thought you were working on that explosiveness?"

"Not when it comes to witches like you."

"Gee, he doesn't have that problem with me," I said, feigning a pensive look as I stepped forward to stand by Dustin's side.

"That's because you don't know him like I do, sweetie." She kept her eyes glued to Dustin, a knowing smile on her face as she lowered her chin, as if challenging Dustin to prove her wrong.

"I know him pretty well."

"Obviously not, or you wouldn't be with him. Or did he say he loves you?" She smirked at me. I wouldn't be sidetracked. Time to focus on the matter at hand.

"My necklace is why I am here. Not your oh-so-riveting conversation. I want it back, now."

"Claudia," Dustin took another step forward, slowly this time. "Give her the necklace. You have stuff to settle? Fine. But it's with me, not her."

"But don't you see? I used the necklace to get you here. This was all part of my plan." She shifted her attention from Dustin back to me. "I have something you want, and you have something I want. It's a trade."

"What do you want?" I asked. I was almost afraid to know her answer. Dustin was the only thing I knew of that I had that she

80

may want. A woman who went through such a cowardly farce to get the attention of an ex-boyfriend was not someone I would ever trust. Especially not when it came to a trade.

"I want Dustin," she said simply with a shrug of one shoulder.

"What?!" Dustin looked flabbergasted. After the bad breakup, I imagine he never would've guessed she'd say those words. I grabbed hold of his hand, intertwining our fingers and I saw that my actions angered her as much as I had hoped.

"Well, sorry, but you can't have him. Or my necklace." I released his hand and charged forward, ready to land a punch right to her chest. Unfortunately, there was one detail Dustin had left out. When he had called her a witch, I didn't realize he had meant that *literally*.

She blocked my punch with her magic. "You little fool." She raised a hand and I began to levitate.

"Put her down, Claudia. You want me? Here I am. Just leave her alone!"

"Put me down, Claudia!" I shouted at the same time as Dustin before grunting as I struggled to get out of her spell. "How about you and me? We fight fair. No magic powers, no other people or special little things helping us out. Just you and me. Any type of non-magic fight you want. You win, you get whatever you want. I win? I get my necklace back and you leave Dustin alone. Forever. Got it?"

She took a moment to consider my offer. "Fine hunter," she slowly lowered me to the floor. "I will fight against you." She used her magic to force Dustin into the chair she had been sitting in and to tie ropes around him.

"Son of a –"

"Oh, shut up. I'll be with you soon, once I'm done with your little *girlfriend*." She said the last word scathingly.

"So, what'll it be, Claudia? Sword fight? Guns? Bowling?"

"Oh, I like the nice fist fights." She used her magic to jump high into the air, kicking me to the ground as she landed. I grunted a bit as I stood back up.

"No magic or the deal is off."

"You really are in no position to make demands," she said as she ran in, taking a swing towards my jaw. I ducked easily at the last moment and let her hit the wall. As she turned, I was right there, spinning a kick into her stomach. She dropped to the floor and spun around, sweeping my legs out from under me. As I fell, I grabbed her ankles and gave a yank, bringing her to the floor as well. I sat on top of her and let my anger loose, landing punches anywhere I could, until she resorted back to magic to fling me off and across the room. She lunged towards me and landed a punch to my stomach, knocking the wind out of me. It was at that point that it devolved into a full on cat fight. I grabbed her hair with one hand and pulled, yanking her head backwards and grabbing her arm with my other hand, chomping my teeth into her skin.

She howled in pain and slapped me across the face with her free hand, to which I responded by releasing her arm and backhanding her.

"You will *never*," backhand, "have Dustin, and you *will*," another slap across the face, "give me back my necklace!"

"Oh, *I* don't want Dustin," she cackled. "The Count does."

I released her and sat back with a small gasp. "Vito… what does he want with him?" Had we tempted fate too much with our relationship? Had the Count finally decided he had had enough and it was time to get rid of Dustin because I dared to have feelings for him? Just like last time? My hands found their way to Claudia's neck without me even realizing it. She flashed fangs at me and laughed.

"What did he want the last time, Kel? This was never about you. It was always about Dustin."

"What does he want with Dustin?"

She used her magic to set herself free and fling me across the room again. She sauntered toward me with a smirk. "In short? Just to kill him."

"No," I struggled to catch my breath. The last hit to the floor was a doozy. "Please… let me go in his place." I was right. Vito wanted to kill Dustin now because I had started to love him. It would be like middle school all over again. I couldn't let that happen.

"Foolish girl, he doesn't want you. Just Dustin."

I looked over to Dustin and saw him wriggling around. He gave me a look that told me he was almost free. I just had to keep her distracted, and then I'd have my hunting partner to help me.

"Why? Why does he want Dustin? At least tell me."

"How should I know why he wants Dustin? Probably because he got Dustin's brother a few years ago, and Dustin now took something from him. Maybe he wants to settle the score. End the feud. "

"His brother?" I knew Dustin had said he and his brother were in a hunting clan together, but he hadn't told me more than that.

"Aww, he never told you about Adam, huh?"

"Adam? What about him?"

"Like I said. How well do you know him? How well do you know his dark past? Do you know what makes him frightened at night or why he can't sleep? What about how to touch him to make him feel at ease with the world?"

"Then tell me, Claudia. You really know him so well? Why can't he sleep at night? What makes him so frightened?" I struggled to get back on my feet.

She laughed a cold, cruel laugh. "It's because of the fact that he blames himself for his brother's death. He was there when Adam died. He saw the Count kill him. He swore he'd take something from Count Vito, and he has. Now the Count will do what it takes to get it back. Even kill Dustin." She placed a hand around my neck. I still hadn't regained enough strength to stand up completely yet, so she pinned me against the wall. "Dustin sees that night every time he goes to sleep. It haunts him to this day, because he wasn't man enough to slay Vito when he had the chance that night. He didn't have the stomach for it. He ran away instead."

"No," I faltered. "That's not true."

"Dustin is a failure to the hunters. He never amounted to anything, and this just proves it."

"But what about you? I thought the two of you had something?" I struggled to get the words out. Her hold on my throat was cutting off oxygen, making it hard to talk and my head felt wobbly. *If I don't get her off my throat now, I'm going to end up passing out.*

"There was never any love there," she spat and released my throat. Her release seemed unwilling. "It was the only way I could get in good with the group."

"So you used him so you could get into the group?" I gasped for air, trying to calm my oxygen starved brain.

"Yes, I used him. I told him I loved him just so I could get Adam and Dustin close to Vito. Why do you think I pretended to be captured by Vito? All so Dustin and his brother would come running to save poor me." Her voice was dripping in disdain.

"What a horrible creature. It must haunt you," I managed to stagger to a standing position. "To know that you had to use someone to get into the group for that? Yet, someone like me could make it in the group and not have to be in love with him to do so?"

"I'd hardly call it being in love with him," she laughed scathingly.

"And why work for Vito now?"

"Oh, we've had a give and take relationship for years. Who do you think taught him how to enter houses without a sound? And how to use his mind control over longer distances?"

"You're the reason he can enter my house unnoticed? And my mind from wherever?" Most elite vampires had to be in fairly close proximity to their victim in order to control their minds and enter their thoughts. Vito was different, and I had no idea as to why his powers were so much more refined. Until now.

I glanced over at Dustin, who briefly paused from his struggle to look at me, shock clearly written all over his face. I hadn't told him about Vito being in my mind before. I definitely couldn't tell him I've spoken back to Vito in the same fashion. I glared at her. "I should've been hunting you from day one as well."

"Oh please, Kel. You know you want the Count, too. He's a true man, with power and money."

"Power and money are not what make a man. Feelings, emotions, caring for people. Having a heart. *Those* are things that make a true man."

"And let me guess," she laughed as I stumbled. "Dustin claims to have all of those? He uses that to get all the women."

"He didn't use anything to get me to love him. I just do."

"Naïve girl. You have no idea what love really is."

"And you do?" I silently hoped that Dustin would finally free himself soon. Ropes tied with magic were always more difficult to break free from, but I had no idea how much longer I could keep her going.

"Dustin took my love away a long time ago."

"You mean… he was a vampire?" My eyes widened at the realization.

"Yes. It was all a game, *Kel*. And it's the same game that Dustin is playing with you. He's using you to get at what he wants."

"Then what is it he wants?"

"He knew Vito was attracted to you. It wasn't hard to figure out why Vito announced that female hunters should be brought to him unharmed the same week that you graduated the Academy. You were the only female hunter in that graduating class. So he stayed with you to get at the Count. And once he's done with Vito, he'll leave. I'm a witch. It has been foretold."

"We are in charge of our own destinies. The vampire you loved. Would you have done anything for him? Even die?"

She stopped ranting and looked dead at me now. "Yes. I would have gladly died for him."

"Then you know how I feel. I've offered my life in exchange for his."

"It doesn't work that way, *hunter*," she spat at me. "You die, he dies. End of story."

"I don't think so, Claudia," Dustin charged and grabbed hold of Claudia, holding his boot knife to her throat. "Now you tell your Count this: if he wants me, he can come and get me. But leave Kel outta this. Kel," he nodded at me. I walked up to Claudia, trying desperately not to stumble and look as confused as I felt, and removed my necklace from her neck.

"Now you tell your Count what I said," he said as he dragged Claudia to the backdoor and threw her outside, slamming the door shut and locking it before turning towards me. "Let's go home," he said as he offered his hand. I took it and offered to drive as the tears welled up in his eyes. I decided in that moment that I'd give him the night, and tomorrow he'd have to tell me everything.

~That's right, hunter. Find out his secrets. Then you will know if you truly love him or not.~

Goodnight, Vito. This is between me and Dustin. Leave it be. I relayed as much sternness in my thoughts as I could muster. Tomorrow could be a game changer, and I needed my thoughts to be my own.

Chapter 10

The next morning I woke up sore. Getting thrown around the room via magic tends to do that. Way more forceful than a person using their physical abilities. I looked at the clock and saw it was well after ten in the morning before getting up and dragging myself to the bathroom to shower. A warm shower always felt good on sore muscles. The steam began to fill the small room as I sat in the bathtub and let the water wash over me. Instead of focusing my thoughts, I allowed them to flow freely this morning.

This is going to be a tough discussion to have with Dustin. How is he doing? What Claudia said last night had to have hurt. Claudia... what did she mean when she said Vito didn't want me, but Dustin? And.... what was it? I die, Dustin dies, end of story? Was the promise not to harm Dustin no longer valid because I ran away? That would make sense. But now Vito no longer cares to protect me now that I abandoned him at his castle that night? Vito. What does he know about Dustin that I don't know? Something important enough to make him confident I may stop loving Dustin, that's for sure.

I finished in the shower, dried off and dressed before trudging downstairs to find some food. I could feel bruising all over my body, and a hot shower wasn't going to do anything for that. As I approached the bottom of the stairs, I could hear Dustin crying. My stomach would have to wait. I stood behind the sofa and laid a hand on his shoulder.

"Dustin? You ok?" It was a stupidly obvious question with an even more obvious answer – of course he wasn't ok. But how else could I broach the subject of last night?

He looked up at me, tears still falling down his cheeks. It startled me a bit – I had never seen him so vulnerable, so… broken. "Yeah, I think so," he said with a steadying breath.

"I don't think so." I wiped the tears from his eyes and walked around to the front of the sofa to sit next to him. "We should talk about last night."

"Yeah. It's just the whole thing. I mean, I finally know the truth, and it hurts. Although probably not quite as bad as you hurt right now. You took a beating last night. How bad are your injuries?"

"My body will heal. Which part of the truth hurts?"

"The fact that I was used." He breathed a heavy sigh. "It doesn't matter anymore. I need to move on. I know the truth now. No more wondering. Now it's time to live with it."

"Dustin," I started. I couldn't do it. I couldn't ask him the questions I wanted to right now. He was sitting here next to me, broken. I couldn't ask questions that may only break him down more. "Come here," I said and pulled him into a gentle hug, so as not to hurt myself too much. "It'll be ok. That's the past, and you have a future that doesn't include her." *Does he? Really?* I couldn't help wondering if Claudia was going to be a main feature in our lives for the foreseeable future. Should I be giving him what might be a false hope? *Well, it's not like you said when in the future it won't include her. Shut up, brain.*

He nodded. "Yeah, you're right."

"Am I ever wrong?" I said with a wink, to which he chuckled. "See? You're feeling a little better already. Did you sleep at all last night?"

"No, not really. I… couldn't." I read his hesitation this time. He tried to sleep but had nightmares again. Were they about the day his brother was killed? He stood with another sigh. It was weighing heavily on his mind. "I'm going to take some medicine for the pain and lay down. Maybe I can sleep this time. G'night, Kel. I'll see you in a few hours or so."

I nodded. "G'night." He went to the kitchen for the medicine, then trudged up the stairs, his footfalls thudding heavily, giving away just how exhausted he was. I sat there on the sofa and turned on the TV, not really paying attention to it.

I hope everything works out. I told him it'd be ok. I really hope I'm not wrong. Claudia was strong. Claudia... hmm... A memory flashed in my mind. *She had fangs! So Dustin's information was right. She IS a vampire. But, also a witch?* I had never heard of such an instance occurring, but I guess it was possible. I had to believe so – the proof wasn't only in front of my eyes last night, but throwing me around like a ragdoll. I kept replaying the night for a good ten or fifteen minutes before deciding it was useless. I went upstairs instead to check on Dustin.

Peeking into his room, I could see him twitching in his sleep. *He usually looks so peaceful when I come in, but right now he looks so tormented.* I placed a soft kiss on his forehead. He groaned and opened his eyes slowly.

"Kel...? Is something wrong? What's-"

"Nothing. I was just worried about you and wanted to make sure you're ok. You didn't look like you were sleeping well." I looked away and bit my lower lip. Not sleeping well was a far cry from the evident torment he was enduring.

"I wasn't." He sat up in bed and gestured for me to sit next to him. I obliged, but slowly. My fear had always been that if I allowed myself to love someone, they'd be in danger because of Vito. Our current situation was far beyond anything I could have imagined.

"What Claudia said yesterday is really bugging me. I really do love you, Kel. I don't want her words to take that away."

I allowed myself a small smile. Even after the tortuous events of last night, his biggest concern was if I still loved him? "There's no way that *she* can take away my love for you, Dustin."

~You're not being entirely truthful, my dear hunter.~ My breath caught.

How long have you been listening? Don't you have something better to do?

~Long enough, my dear. And there is nothing more important to me than you. It's time you realize that.~

"What's wrong?" Dustin looked at me, concerned. I couldn't tell him the battle going on inside my mind right now. He had enough to think about already.

"Nothing, just sore from last night. Listen, I love you, Dustin. And neither Claudia nor Vito can take away that love."

He looked at me as his eyes started tearing up again. "I believe you," he whispered.

Now's the time. Now or never. "Dustin, will you tell me about your past?"

"Uh, ok… what would you like to know?"

"Anything you're willing to tell me. I know practically nothing about you from before we met."

"Well, let's see. It's pretty normal up until about 16, when my brother joined a vampire hunting team. I wanted to join him, but he wouldn't let me. My father didn't want me to, either. It wasn't until one night, the day after I turned 17, that a local hospital was being overrun with vamps. Our grandmother was there at the time because of a stroke. The vampires came in and started attacking the patients and staff. My brother and his team, led by a guy named L.T., went in and started to clean out the vamps. Well, they had reached the floor that my grandmother was on. I happened to be visiting her at the time. There was no place to run or hide. One of my brother's team members was killed outside her room. The vamp tried to enter the room, but I was able to knock him through an adjacent wall. I picked up the fallen hunter's weapon and slew my first vamp in order to save my grandmother. L.T. saw the whole thing and made me a member, against my brother's wishes. That's how I got into hunting. I was already taking courses at the hunting academy, but my dad and brother had plans on me becoming a professor, not a hunter. That night changed everything."

"But… where did Vito come into this whole mess?" *It's obvious there's old history between Dustin and Vito. Vito hasn't been after Dustin just because of me. There's more to it.*

~Much more, hunter.~

"Vito showed up a few months later." Dustin looked past me as he recalled his past. "Claudia had just gotten into the group. Claudia and I got involved with each other, then she got captured. Or, pretended to, I guess. Adam, Lance, and I went to go get her back. Before we got to Vito's front door, Lance went down. There was a fight between some demons and us for what seemed like hours. Adam and I busted through the door and found Claudia chained up in the basement. Vito was there waiting for us. Adam charged Vito as I set Claudia free. Adam told her and me to get outta there."

He closed his eyes and dropped his head. "I was defiant, but he made me leave. As we headed up the stairs, I looked back at Adam. Just as I looked back, Adam was killed. He was watching to make sure we left, and Vito killed him right there. I screamed, full of pain and hatred. All I had left was my knife, so I charged and I stabbed Vito with it. It was made of pure silver, so it burned where I stabbed his arm. It gave Claudia and me enough time to run."

"Claudia said you killed her love. It was that vampire you killed that night at the hospital, wasn't it?"

"I guess so. It was the only time I'd ever killed anyone or anything. I didn't even know about that until last night."

"Claudia also said you took something from Vito. What was it?"

"Judging from last night? I'd say it's you."

I placed my hand on his, watching the tears flow down his face, agonized. I felt the tears forming in my eyes as well, and tried to blink them away so Dustin wouldn't see.

"It's my fault that Adam's gone."

"No, it's not your fault. He died because he wanted you safe, and to live your life. To be happy with who you are. He wouldn't want you to feel sorry for yourself. Or guilty."

He nodded, slowly. "Yeah… I guess you're right." He wiped the tears from his eyes. "I'm sure he would have loved to have met you, Kel."

I smiled. "Remember the good times, Dustin. Don't focus on the bad ones." *I should take my own advice. I remember some of the good times with my parents, too, but the memory that comes up most often is… that night.*

"Thank you, Kel. You give me so much comfort when I feel so alone."

"That's because I love you. And I will always be here whenever you need me."

"I love you, too, Kel." He leaned forward and kissed my cheek before yawning.

"Get some sleep now, ok? I'll stay until you fall asleep," I said with a yawn. The few hours of sleep I had gotten weren't good ones, and I felt the full weight of exhaustion now.

Dustin held up the covers. "There's plenty of space, you know." I skootched under the covers, too tired to speak now. The last thing I remember was Dustin laying an arm over me as I drifted off. The next thing I knew, I had a sudden chill and my eyes snapped open.

"Dustin?" I whispered and looked over to him, breathing a sigh of relief. "It was only a bad dream. That's all," I whispered reassuringly to myself.

"Hm? What's wrong Kel?"

"Nothing, I was just wondering if you were asleep or not."

"Not anymore."

"Sorry." I felt the cool night breeze on my face. We had managed to sleep the whole day away. "Did you leave the window open?"

"No… I figured you did." He opened his eyes fully and sat up. "If I didn't open it, and you didn't…"

"Maybe… the wind blew it open?" I tried to sound hopeful, but I was filled with doubt. The wind doesn't just blow these windows open.

"Yeah, that's it," Dustin said as he grabbed his flashlight off his night stand. "The wind did it." He turned the flashlight on and got out of bed. After the nightmare I had just woken from, I didn't trust my legs to hold me up. He grabbed a firearm from the nightstand drawer and began searching the room, putting a finger to his lips to remind me to stay quiet. I nodded and grabbed my necklace. After the last incident, I wanted to make sure it was still there, and sure enough the nice, cold metal reassured me that it was safely around my neck.

After he was satisfied that his bedroom was clear, he made his way across the hall, to my room. I sat up and focused my attention on listening for anything that sounded off, readying myself to jump into action if needed. Nothing. I heard him make his way to the bathroom. Down the stairs. The living room, then the kitchen. Down to the basement where the gym was. And then I heard nothing until I heard the soft footfalls on the staircase.

"Nothing amiss," he reported.

"Ok. Will you close the window now?"

He walked over and shut it tight, locking it in place. "All done," he said as he crawled back into bed.

"Thank you."

"Try to relax and sleep, ok?"

I nodded. "I'll try to relax, but I'm not promising anything about sleep." I laid my head on his chest and listened for a moment to his breathing, which was finally starting to slow down.

"Dustin? If I ask you to leave me, and it's for your own good, will you please promise me you'll go? And continue life. Don't let me slow you down."

"What?" He turned his head toward me. "I don't understand."

"Please… just promise me that if I ask you to leave, please go. I would only tell you to go if it's for your own good."

"No, I won't leave you when you need me the most." He wrapped an arm around my shoulder. I couldn't stop the tears from overflowing. The nightmare I had felt so real, and the only way to save Dustin was to make him leave on his own. He wouldn't go, so he was… killed. I didn't even want to bring the thought to mind.

"Please, Dustin. Promise me that if something ever happens to me, you'll continue your life."

"But Kel, nothing's going to happen to you."

"We're hunters, Dustin. You can't know that. Promise me. Please?"

"Yes… I promise." His voice was full of hesitation. "Kel, just sleep. No more talk tonight."

"Ok," I nodded as I focused my energy on stopping the tears.

"I won't let go tonight," were the last words I heard him say before I drifted back off into unconsciousness.

Chapter 11

THUD!

"Owwww...." I sat up sleepily as I opened my bleary eyes and turned them upward towards the bed, Dustin looking down at me with an amused look.

"Well, that's one way to get out of bed."

I squinted my eyes at him, trying to give him a dirty look through the sleepiness I still felt. "Oh hush." He extended a hand down to me.

"Are you ok? Need a hand?"

"Yeah, I'll be ok," as I took his hand and stood. "I'm going to get dressed and go get some water."

Downstairs, I decided after a sip of water to do some stretching. I needed a day to relax, but also needed some exercise. One top priority for a hunter was staying in peak physical shape. I sat on the floor in the living room and started doing some gentle stretches. Dustin came down the stairs, whistling a tune. He donned a pair of blue jeans and a blue t-shirt, which was a far cry from the usual hunter attire of dark and subdued colors. It also made me immediately suspicious, since he didn't deviate from the dark colors often.

"Hey, sup?"

"Nothing much," he said with a big smile before heading to the fridge. "How about you?"

"Well, I was thinking about breaking out the gaming console. Play some dancing games and get some exercise, ya know?"

"Yeah, that sounds like fun." He poured himself a glass of soda. "Or…" he took a sip. "Or we could head down to the mall. I feel like shopping."

I cocked my head at him. "Really?" Shopping wasn't really Dustin's thing, unless it was for new hunter gear, and that was something we couldn't get at the mall.

"Yeah, really. I don't know. I've been so uptight lately, I figured I need a break."

I jumped up and grabbed my sneakers by the front door. "Let's go! Whatever's gotten into you though, I want to know. You sure it's just needing a break?" I asked as I tied my shoes. He took another sip of soda before putting down the glass and approaching me, taking my hand into his, rubbing it gently with his fingertips.

"Well, with you around, yeah I think a break would be good every once in a while. Unless you have a better idea on how to get my mind off things?"

I grinned. "Well, I *do* have ideas, *but…* you'll have to earn them." I winked playfully.

"Hmm. I might like the sound of that."

I grinned wider. "Well, you either do, or you don't. But if you don't wanna know, then maybe you don't want to do it…" And queue the sad puppy dog eyes.

"Well, I think I wanna know." He laughed.

"Well, there's a DDR machine in the mall, as you know. And we used to have a routine for the machine that they have, and I heard there's a tournament tomorrow. Do the tournament, and I think I can get you to loosen up." I beamed. This was the only form of dancing I had ever seen Dustin do. In fact, he was the one who introduced me to the game: Dance Dance Revolution. It was early on in our partnership, and he had told me it would help build trust. He wasn't wrong.

He considered my proposal carefully. "Hmm… sure, I can give it a shot."

"Really?!"

He shrugged. "Well, I haven't been in a tourney before, but… well, why not?"

I jumped up, almost hitting him in my excitement, and gave him a big hug. He wasn't one for being the center of attention, unless it was when we were hunting vampires, so I was really surprised he agreed without putting up a fight. "Oh, Dustin, thank you! I haven't been in one before either, but I've seen them online… ooooh, this is gonna be great! Oh yeah, we got to go shopping for outfits for us to wear. We'll do that today while we're at the mall."

I don't know what's going on, but I think I might be able to enjoy this new Dustin for a bit. As long as he doesn't have something up his sleeve that I should be worried about, of course.

"Umm, ok… as long as I'm not wearing a spaghetti strap and a skirt, I should be fine. I think." He snapped my shirt strap to emphasize his point.

"Nah, I'll find something that'll look good on you." I winked. *Not like that's hard. Hunters are lean and muscular. He'd look good in just about anything. Wait, focus. Tournament.*

I grabbed the keys and tossed them to Dustin. He caught them and grabbed his sunglasses from the table by the door and headed out to the car. On the way out, I double checked to ensure I locked the door. After the window incident, I didn't want to take any chances.

Speaking of taking chances… I hopped in the front seat and Dustin took off, shades and a smile on his face. *I hope I don't regret taking the chance to ask this now.*

"So, Dustin. What's with this whole change of attitude thing? I mean, yesterday you were the usual you, but today…? You're different."

"Hm," he grinned. "I think maybe I got hit in the head kinda hard by a demon last night while searching the house." He laughed. "Actually, Kel, I have no idea. But right now, I feel a lot less stressed."

"Ok," I nodded. "That's good."

"Yup, that it is."

"Stress is *not* a human's best friend."

"Nope. Wait. Are you calling me human?" He raised an eyebrow at me playfully.

"Well sure, why not?"

He shrugged. "Ok, I can deal with that."

"Are you telling me you're something other than human?" I smirked.

"Maybe," he said playfully. "Kidding. Only kidding."

"Uh-huh, yeah. Sure you were," I laughed. It felt good to laugh. Before I knew it, we arrived at the mall. When was the last time we came here and just chilled? It felt like forever, with all of the recent events going on. *Nope, don't think about what's been going on lately. Today is you, Dustin, and the DDR machine. Nothing else.* "Chaaaaaarge!" I shouted as I opened my door, causing Dustin to look at me, feigning fear.

"Oh dear lord, maybe this wasn't a good idea."

I went around the car and grabbed his hand before he could back out. "You said you want to loosen up, remember?"

"Very much so, and after this I might need it."

We walked around the mall and looked around at outfits, not having much luck in finding matching ones, but a lot of fun and distraction, which was exactly what we needed. We stopped for lunch and then continued the search, until we walked right by the arcade. I stopped and walked backwards before turning into the storefront and grabbing some tokens for the DDR machine.

"Oh boy," Dustin laughed. "Here we go."

I laughed as I put in enough tokens for both of us. "Ready to play some 'Dance Dance Revolution?'" I asked in my best announcer voice. Dustin rolled his eyes as he stepped up to the second player dance pad. My plan thus far had worked. He'd relaxed and hopefully forgotten about… her. I selected a song and difficulty and hit start. As the music began, however, I had to do a double take at the group of people already forming around us, and almost missed my first step.

"Whoa. I could have sworn I know that face."

"Probably a friend of yours," Dustin replied, focusing on the screen.

"Yeah, probably," I conceded. I sang along to the music while dancing, glancing around again as soon as I had the chance, but not seeing the face again. *I don't think that was one of my friends. I don't have very many.*

I let Dustin choose the last two songs, each of us taking sips of water in between, which gave me the chance to glance around every so often, and I didn't see the face again, although a crowd had now gathered around to watch us. We finished our game and left the arcade laughing, arm in arm. As my breathing slowed back down, my mind flashed back to the face. *I really hope that wasn't who I think it was.*

"Dustin?"

"Hm?"

"What do you think the possibility is of me seeing someone I know here? I mean, most people I know are hunters, and it's not like any of us frequent the mall."

He gave it a moment of thought before he seemed to come to a conclusion that seemed plausible. "Well, maybe it just looked like someone familiar."

I nodded, not fully convinced. "Yeah, that's probably what it was." I was probably just being paranoid because of recent events, which was no surprise.

As we came up to one of the big department stores, I dragged Dustin in to look for more outfits for the next day's tournament. After a few minutes, I didn't see Dustin anywhere anymore. *Ah well, he probably wandered off to see what he could find.* I kept browsing the racks, not really pleased with anything I was finding, and my mind still a bit distracted by the idea that I could've possibly seen Claudia here.

What brought me out of my distraction was my cell phone ringing. I picked up as soon as I saw it was Dustin.

"Hello?"

"Help, I'm lost."

I laughed. "Figures. Where are you?"

"Ummm…. next to a mannequin wearing some silk underwear and the dressing rooms."

I couldn't stop myself from busting into laughter now. "Oh geeze, now that *really* figures. Alright, stay there. I'll come find you." It didn't take me long to locate him and decide to give him a start. I snuck up behind him and grabbed his sides with a squeeze. He jumped and turned around sharply to stare at me, hand to his chest as he struggled to get his breath under control.

"Geeze, Kel, you gave me a heart attack!"

"Serves you right for getting lost in the lingerie section," I snickered. "And just what were you looking for?"

He pointed to himself, "I was just looking for some clothing for you and took a wrong turn."

"Mm-hmm. Well, the clothing that we're supposed to be looking at is right over there." I grabbed his arm and led him away. "See anything in there you like?" I tried so hard not to laugh as he started blushing again.

"Umm… no." When he looked at me smirking with my eyebrows raised, he added, "well, there were a few things…"

That one caught me by surprise, since I didn't expect him to own up to it. I was actually grateful when I happened upon a red shirt that looked comfortable enough to dance in. "Hey! Let's see if we can find one in the men's section for you. We can match it with black pants. Simple, yet bold."

I dragged him off to the men's department to find a matching shirt without giving him a chance to answer. I wasn't sure I wanted to hear any more about what he saw that he may have liked. He went to grab a pair of black pants that allowed room for dancing in while I headed to the counter for us to pay. I paid for the clothes and he grabbed the bag, heading out of the store quickly.

"What's with you? You look like you've seen a ghost or something. Are you that embarrassed about being lost in the lingerie section?"

"Who, me? Nah, I'm ok," he said with a shrug. "Just ready to be out of here." I wasn't convinced, but decided to drop the subject.

"Well, we have enough time for another round of DDR. Hit up the game room on the way back to the car?"

"Sure."

As we approached the game room, I came to a halt. "Dustin?" I nudged his arm. "Who does that look like to you?" *Please don't be her. Please let me be imagining things.*

"Who?" He looked at the girl on the dance pad with purple hair bouncing around. "N… no, I don't know."

"Are you sure?"

"Yeah, the hair just threw me for a moment."

"Who did you think it could be?"

"Oh, I thought it was…" the woman on the dance pad shifted around just enough for us to see her face. Dustin's face went pale as he whispered the name "Claudia."

"Yeah, that's what I thought, too. And we're gone. Now," I grabbed Dustin's arm to lead him away as he looked at me with a face that said "I'm gonna be sick." *She saw us. I know she did. We can't do this here. Not with so many innocent people around.*

"Dustin, are you ok?" His face looked like he was fighting some internal battle. Made me think of the times I fought to get Vito out of my mind.

"Yes… yes, I'm fine. I don't think she saw us. Let's just leave."

Without another word, we headed straight for the doors that would take us outside to fresh air and our car. *Why would she be there? Doesn't she have some evil plot to be working on? Did she know we were going to be there? If she did, how? And would she attack in a mall full of innocent bystanders?*

Back at home, I unlocked the door and walked in quietly. Dustin followed behind, setting the bag of clothing on the floor by the door.

"I have a headache. I'm going to go take some meds and a nap."

I nodded. "Nap sounds good to me, too."

"Ok, I'll see you in a bit." We both trudged up the stairs and into our own rooms. I flopped down onto my bed, face first, wondering the same questions about Claudia over and over again, until I finally fell asleep.

I woke up a couple of hours later, hearing Dustin's voice. I got up and went to his room to see what was going on, but he was still asleep.

"No… get away from her. It's not her you want. No!!!" He bolted into a sitting position, panting heavily.

"Dustin? It's ok, it was just a dream." He gazed in my direction, his eyes slowly focusing on me.

"Yeah, just a dream. A bad dream." He ran his fingers through his damp hair, then wiped the sweat from his forehead with the back of his hand.

"Still worried about Claudia?"

"Honestly? Yes," he sighed, his face falling into a look of hopelessness. "I'm worried that I'll lose you to something you had no part in."

"I'm here for you, Dustin." I took the necklace with my ring from around my neck, now fastening the clip around his neck. "See this ring? As long as you have this ring, I'm with you."

He gently touched the ring before placing it safely under his shirt. "Are you sure you want me to have this? I know what it means to you."

"Then you know what you mean to me. Come on, how about we go practice for tomorrow? It'll give us something else to focus on."

He nodded and slowly followed me downstairs to dance. We spent the rest of the evening practicing our routine and playing other video games to relax. It must've worked for him, since he fell asleep on the sofa. The lyrics to our song kept running through my head though.

"I need your love in every way, and I feel this every day, 'cause I have too many tears to fall in love again." Why did we have to pick this song? It was before I developed any feelings, sure. But now? It just hits so close to home. I gazed over at Dustin as my eyes finally got too heavy to keep open.

Chapter 12

"I'm really excited Dustin… and kind of nervous." It had taken me all morning to assure myself that seeing Claudia yesterday was a fluke. That she wouldn't be there again today.

"Same here," he gave me a reassuring look. "We'll do fine. I'm sure of it."

"It's our turn. Ready?"

"I think so." Despite trying to help calm my nerves, he looked nervous as could be.

I nodded. "Let's go, before we both back out. Our reputation would be destroyed if people found out a couple of hunters chickened out." I laughed and reached out to grab hold of Dustin's hand so he couldn't back away, and led him up to the dance pad. After a few seconds, I found our song and selected it. We danced our routine flawlessly, and at the end of the song, I planted a kiss square on his lips for extra effect and gave him a wink. The audience burst into applause as we stepped off the dance pad.

"Now, how was *that* for a performance, hm? We rocked it!"

"That was very interesting. Enjoyable way to end the dance," he smiled at me and grabbed my hand. We stood back and watched the other competitors, some doing solos, others doing duets. Many were skilled dancers, with one soloist even doing a backflip on the dance pad. I took to running my fingers through my hair, twirling it from time to time. A nervous habit.

"Geeze, they're kinda good, aren't they?"

I glanced up briefly at the couple on the dance pad before going back to my hair. "Hm? Oh, yeah, I guess so." I glanced back up as the next couple – the last ones, finally! – took the dance pad. As I began to turn my eyes away again, my head whipped over to their direction. It couldn't be... *them*. On the dance pad. What on Earth was a 296 year old vampire doing in an arcade playing a dancing game? If I wasn't so nervous about a potentially deadly scene, I might've outright laughed.

"D... Dustin. Is that who I think it is?"

He looked up at the couple and his face went pale as his jaw dropped. He tried to make a sound, but nothing came out. He stood as though frozen in place.

"Please tell me I'm hallucinating." *Not here. Not now. Not with all these innocent people around.* Hunters always tried to keep innocents safe and unaware of the vampires around. If we were to fight now, casualties would be high. The arcade was in a small city, but it was still enough people to not be a hunter town – which meant most of these people had no clue vampires even existed.

"What are they doing here?" His voice was barely audible. He looked at me and must've seen the dread in my face. Was Vito going to snatch me up here, where I couldn't fight back without risking innocent peoples' lives?

"Shh, don't worry about it. I don't think they're going to start trouble here. Too many people. Besides, if they wanted to, they would have already. They could've ambushed us right after we got off the dance pad when we weren't paying attention."

I nodded slowly, trying to slow my racing thoughts. "Yeah, maybe you're right." I could only hope he was. For the first time since I started hunting, I didn't have any of my normal weaponry with me, not even my boot knife, since I was in sneakers today, and now I felt stupid for that. I knew better, and should always have at least a dagger on me.

As Claudia and Vito finished their routine, the crowd broke into applause. I saw Dustin's eye twitch and his mouth contorted with disgust. I could only imagine Claudia was in his mind, as she was looking directly at him. I, on the other hand, glared at Vito, who simply smiled back at me.

~Tut tut, my pet. Everything will be alright. You are safe today.~

What are you doing here? Just... leave me alone, Vito. My thoughts were pleading. I still couldn't help but worry about the people around us, in case a fight did break out. These were normal people. People who had no idea that two vampires, one who was also a witch, were not only standing in front of them, but that they were applauding and cheering for them.

~Oh, I intend to. For now.~

For now?

~I'm here to enjoy myself today, my dear.~

On a dancing game? Really?

~Just because I'm almost three centuries old doesn't mean I don't find enjoyment in life. I rather enjoyed your performance. Most of it, at least.~

The announcer stepped up to the dance pad and began his ending bits, which allowed me to snap my head and mind away from Vito for the moment. Vito had said he enjoyed most of my performance. Of course the part he wouldn't have enjoyed was the kiss at the end. The announcer began with the normal thanks and great job to all participants before moving onto the winners for solo dances.

"And the winning duo for the couples play is... Monte and Brittney!" The audience began to cheer and clap again as the couple stepped up for their prize and I let my breath out as I joined in the applause for the winning couple.

"Oh well. We tried."

Dustin forced a smile at me. "It's ok. You're number one in my book."

I forced a smile back, along with half a laugh. I was still preoccupied by the presence of Claudia and Vito at the tournament. "Thank you, sweetheart. For everything. Especially for putting up with me, practicing the routine so much with such short notice."

He shrugged. "It was nothing. I had fun." He smiled and winked at me.

"I'm sure you did," I laughed. "You ready to go?"

He nodded. "I think so. The sooner, the better."

"Definitely." I held on tight to Dustin's hand and glared once more, this time at both Vito and Claudia, who were both watching us as we made our way out of the arcade. Claudia had a smug look on her face, and Vito had that eternal sadness that almost always seemed to pull at his eyes. Dustin quickened his pace, and I struggled to keep up without jogging, until we got close to the car.

I stopped Dustin as we approached the car and gave him a soft kiss on the lips.

"You're being extra affectionate today." He raised an eyebrow at me.

"It's a thank you. You were wonderful today."

"Well then," he leaned in and kissed me back. "So were you."

Finally back home, I checked every room of the house to make sure nothing was out of order. I knew I was being paranoid. Vito said I was safe today. And as weird as it always was, I trusted him, despite this probably being another mind game of his. Claudia, however, I didn't trust. Finally satisfied, I told Dustin I was going to go lie down for a bit and headed to my room. I wanted a few minutes alone to sort through my thoughts before making dinner. He followed me up the stairs.

"You did a great job today, Kel. That was the most fun we've had in a while."

"Thank you."

He gave me a hug before letting me go to my room, and he made his way to his. I laid in my bed and grabbed my teddy bear. *Why would Vito and Claudia show up there? They knew we were going to be there today, no doubt about it. What is his game this time? Can't he just let me have one thing I can enjoy without him barging in on it?*

I was overcome by exhaustion, seemingly from nowhere. My last thought was Vito – did he have something to do with how I was feeling? Was he hearing my thoughts racing again and want peace? I wouldn't put it past him anymore. Sleep came on quickly, but it wasn't restful.

"No… Vito…. leave us alone! NO! DUSTIN!!!" In my dream I had thrown a large object in the direction of Vito, who was dragging Dustin away, his body limp from a blitz attack. Next thing I knew, I had my dagger in hand and was rushing towards them. "Give him back." I was crying when Vito's hand grabbed my wrist, stopping my dagger attack. I then felt a hand on my shoulder, hearing Dustin's voice as though coming from a ghost.

"Kel, sweetie?"

I opened my eyes and took in my surroundings, my face tear-stricken. Dustin was holding my left shoulder down and had my right wrist in his hand, preventing me from hitting him with the dagger that had been under my pillow.

"Hey, it's ok. It's me." The concern was evident in his face as I took a few calming breaths.

"I'm ok. Sorry about that. Just a bad dream, that's all." He let go of my shoulder and I sat up a bit, when I saw my pillow on the floor across the room. I must've thrown it while dreaming. He let go of my wrist and I placed my dagger back in its position where my pillow would cover it up again.

"It's ok, don't apologize." He wrapped his arms around me as I began to cry on his shoulder freely. *How can I make this relationship work when I'm terrified that Vito will kill him because of me?*

"When did you start keeping a dagger on your bed?"

"Awhile back, after a bad… nightmare. Kind of like this one." No way I could tell him now that it had been after the encounter with Vito when I had been injured.

"It's ok now. Nothing will get you."

"But that's just it. He didn't get me, he got… he got you. I couldn't stand that." Vito killing me had never been a part of any of my nightmares. He told me he'd protect me when I was a child, and now he's told me he wants me for his bride. My fear since middle school was that he would kill anyone else I ever got close to, and I couldn't get much closer to Dustin than I was now.

"Who got me?" His voice was constricted, and I was pretty sure he already knew the answer.

"Him." I swallowed, not even wanting to say his name right now. "Vito. I was so scared. I couldn't do anything to help you."

"Shhh, baby, it's ok. He can't get me. You've got nothing to fear. I'm here right now and he can't touch me. It was a nightmare."

"I know, but it felt so… real. And I was so helpless. I hate that feeling."

"It wasn't real, it was just a dream. You know he can't get me that easily."

"Please just… lie here with me? At least until I fall asleep."

"You sure you don't want to get up and eat something?

"No, I feel sick to my stomach right now."

"Ok," he nodded as he climbed onto my bed and held me as I closed my eyes. It was over an hour of lying there quietly before I finally started to fall asleep, feeling his head rest on mine. He was falling asleep, too. *Maybe it's ok to be vulnerable with him.*

I felt Dustin stir and opened my eyes, looking first at the clock and then at Dustin, who was looking at me and smiling softly. It was just after two in the morning. I readjusted in the bed to lay my head on Dustin's chest. *Yes, I can be vulnerable with him.* "Please don't go anywhere. Don't leave me."

"I won't."

"I like this. Sleeping safe and warm in your arms."

"Me, too." He wrapped his arms tighter around me. The thought struck me as funny – here we were, two strong and confident vampire hunters, vulnerable and afraid together. As hunting partners, we were supposed to bring out each other's strengths. And during battles, we did. However, we also brought out each other's weaknesses when we weren't fighting. *Please let us stay strong when we fight. Don't let this be our downfall.*

Chapter 13

I opened my eyes to see soft light passing through the curtains of my room. Morning already. I looked to Dustin's face as I heard his breath, soft and slow. *He's cute when he's sleeping peacefully. I still can't get over how he looks like a little angel when he sleeps.* I stretched some and placed a soft kiss on his forehead before lifting the covers some and sneaking out of bed. I paused as he curled into a ball and wrapped the covers more tightly around himself, then quickly and quietly made my way to the bathroom to shower to avoid waking him up, forgetting to grab clothes.

Making my way back to my room, wrapped in my towel, I crept quietly to my dresser to grab some clean clothes.

"Morning." Dustin's groggy voice made me turn my head quickly, only to chuckle at the sight of Dustin's hair and clothes all askew.

"Morning, sunshine."

"Mm-hmm." He ran his hand through his hair, trying to tame the wild mess atop his head.

"Sleep well?"

A small nod. "Yeah, what about you?"

"Hmmm…. I slept pretty well after you came in." I held the towel tightly to my body and turned back to the dresser to grab clothing quickly, feeling my cheeks get warm. He rubbed the sleep from his eyes so he could focus, and noticed the towel around my body.

"I'm… going to go to the bathroom and let you get dressed in peace."

"Probably a good idea," I nervously laughed as he quickly made his way past me and to the bathroom, his cheeks slightly flushed.

A few minutes later, Dustin popped his head into my doorway. "Want to get your heart racing?"

"Say what?"

"Let's make some breakfast and train today," he winked.

Training sounded like a good idea after feeling so vulnerable yesterday. Training always made me feel more confident, and less at risk. I excelled in many fighting skills, but I really needed to work on some hand to hand combat techniques. My slight stature was often a disadvantage, and I hated to admit it. I was able to use dance and acrobatics to help even the playing field some, but I could still be overpowered easier than I cared to admit. "Sounds like a plan. Be right there." I finished tidying up in my room and gave my teddy bear a quick hug before putting him back on my shelf next to my doll and heading downstairs to the kitchen with a pleasurable inhale.

"I smell meat," I said appreciatively.

"Protein packed breakfast."

I gave an approving nod. Helps to build the muscle, which couldn't hurt. After breakfast we went down to the basement to train. I knew I wasn't a real good match for Dustin, but we practiced hand to hand anyway, giving me a chance to practice some new take downs. I even managed to pin Dustin a few times.

Drenched in sweat, we agreed it was time for a cool down and to stretch out the muscles. I settled into some lunges, followed by splits and straddles. I knew my flexibility and agility were my greatest strengths, and I wasn't going to ignore them and let them falter. I looked over at Dustin, who had taken to doing some one handed push-ups.

"Show off," I joked.

"Oh shut up. There are things you can do that I can't. Like that extra stretchy crap." He rolled his eyes at me before going back to softly counting his push-ups. It wasn't a bad idea, I conceded, so I began my push-up exercises, too. I had modified the pushups in order to work the different muscle groups. Dustin finished his workout and grabbed his water from the table, watching me continue while he hydrated. I dropped to the floor, exhausted but feeling satisfied, as he walked over with a towel for me to wipe the sweat from my face.

"Thanks," I wiped the sweat from my brow and stood to start practicing some dance and acrobatic moves that often came in handy during fights, focusing on adding power to the moves. I had been lucky in some ways while growing up. A dance teacher took pity on me and let me join her classes for free. I never danced on stage or anything, but the movement was a good outlet for me.

"Don't you think you've done enough, Kel?" He raised his eyebrow at me.

"Nope. Gotta go all out. Get better. Stronger."

"Well, today's my easy day." Another sip of water. "I guess that's fine, if you think your body can handle it."

"It'll handle it, whether it wants to or not."

Dustin walked up to me and forced me to stop for a moment. "Kel, what's this about?"

I bit my lip and looked away before answering. "Yesterday…" I sighed and looked up at Dustin. "I felt vulnerable. I didn't have my weapons, and I know my hand to hand is lacking a bit. And if I have to face Claudia again, I need to be able to knock her out quick so she can't use her magic on me again. I hate feeling vulnerable. But I've been feeling that way a lot lately, and I'm hating myself for it. So I need to get stronger."

I turned from Dustin and walked over to the punching bag, taping a poorly drawn image of Vito and Claudia to it, before attacking it with everything I had left in me. Dustin came over to hold the bag and give me a little extra resistance.

"Well, you're obviously pissed. Kel? Kel?" I stopped for a moment and just looked at him. "May I make a suggestion?" A curt nod told him I was listening. "You're dropping your guard when you come in for the jab with your right. Let me give you a few pointers?"

I lost track of the time we spent in the basement. It wasn't easy to accept help, but I knew I needed to get over it and get better, no matter the cost. The cost for not improving could be much greater than swallowing my pride right now. And Dustin was definitely much better at hand to hand combat than I was. Several times I let my anger get the best of me, and Dustin had to stop me, which of course frustrated me even more.

"You're fighting blind with rage again."

"Ugh." I growled. "Better to do it now than when actually fighting against vamps, isn't it?" This had to be at least the third time he told me that. I was angry with myself more than anything. I wanted to work through my rage, but I also knew it would serve me no purpose in a fight. And that's what this training was for – being ready for fights.

"You know what you practice in here is what you'll do in a real fight. Let's adjust your feet first for better balance," he moved around the punching bag and adjusted my feet. "Now, bring your left arm up like this," he gently pulled my arm up into place. "Ok, now try again," he encouraged.

I sighed and began attacking the punching bag again, more focused, trying to remember each tip he gave me in order to not succumb to the rage yet again. He made another slight adjustment to my left arm as it started to drop again. I finally had to admit that my body was done for the day. I could barely stand. Dustin nodded and helped guide me back up to the living room, my legs fighting to give out underneath me. I was exhausted, but it felt great. I felt stronger. Less vulnerable, despite feeling weak with exhaustion right now. *I can't let myself feel vulnerable like that again,* I thought as I sank into the sofa.

~You can always feel vulnerable around me, dear hunter.~

Crap. I had been so focused on my physical vulnerability that I let my mind slip and become susceptible to Vito once again. Since the dance contest, I had been working hard on getting my mental walls up first thing in the morning when I woke up, but I just didn't have the energy for that focus right now. I worried that they knew to find us at the mall because he had heard my thoughts. If it wasn't one thing, it was another.

How long have you been listening this time?

~Long enough.~

Never a direct answer with you, is it?

I could almost hear him laughing at me as I worked to tune him out and get my mental defenses back in place. That was always more difficult when I was physically exhausted, and I had truly pushed my body to the brink of full blown exhaustion.

"Everything ok, sweetie?" Dustin handed me a cold bottle of water and sat down next to me, taking a swig from his own bottle.

"Yeah," I sighed. I didn't want to tell him Vito was ever present once again. "I just really wish I could beat the crap out of Vito and Claudia and get it done with."

~You know that's not entirely true my dear.~

Shut up. I refused to admit to myself that I didn't think I could actually face Vito head on. The few rare opportunities I had, I always hesitated and couldn't figure out why. It was like something inside me refused to allow me to face him head on, and I'd always berated myself afterwards.

"I know. Believe me, I know." He nodded and brushed a few stray strands of hair from my face. "We'll both get our chance. I promise."

It was my turn to nod as I sat quietly. I knew we'd get our chance. That wasn't the question. The question was: would I finally be able to do it when I got the chance again? I wanted to be alone with my thoughts, which meant I really needed to focus on the mental walls to get Vito out. Or maybe…

Leave me alone. Please. I need to think in peace. I didn't usually ask him for anything like this. I wasn't even sure it would work. But I figured it was at least worth a try.

~Dah, very well, hunter. Enjoy your thoughts.~

I couldn't believe it worked. I couldn't be sure that he wasn't listening still, but at least the only thoughts in my head now would be my own. I turned to Dustin. "I'm going to go grab a shower. Order a pizza for dinner?"

"I'll make it two," he laughed. After a full day of training, we had missed lunch and were both starving. I smiled and made my way to the bathroom. With both of them gone, I could focus on my thoughts.

As the warm water rushed over my body, it rinsed away the sweat and some of my frustration. Would I be able to face Vito? Claudia wasn't even a question – she made my blood boil and I knew without a doubt I'd be able to fight her. But why did my body always hesitate in a fight with Vito? It was almost like an invisible hand was holding me back each time. How could I overcome that hesitation so I could finally kill my parents' murderer? I needed to avenge them.

Or maybe I felt the need to prove to myself that I could. After all these years of him always being close by, Vito was the only vampire I'd faced that I couldn't kill. It constantly made me question my abilities as a hunter. A true hunter should be able to face off against any vampire they came across. As of yet, I had never been able to land a single blow, never mind get near him with my dagger. Would the next time be any different? My parents had no problems facing off against any vampire. Could I ever live up to their legacy they had left behind?

Chapter 14

I stumbled down the stairs groggily the next morning. Sleep was practically nonexistent, thanks to my mind never shutting up. Dustin was lounging on the sofa, watching some pointless news network – some mundane network that attributed vampire attacks to wild animals or deranged people, so it didn't provide us with much useful information other than the weather. Ignoring him, I made my way to the kitchen to find some medicine. I felt like I had been hit by a truck.

"You ok, sweetie?"

"Eh." I scrunched up my nose as a wave of nausea hit me. "We got anything for nausea?"

"Yeah, in the medicine cabinet in the bathroom, I should have something."

I nodded as slightly as I could to avoid more nausea. "I'm gonna go grab some, ok?"

"Sure." He looked over his shoulder at me. "Actually, you look like you should go lie down." He grabbed me as I tried to take a step and stumbled a bit. "You're burning up. Come on, lay down on the sofa."

"Yeah, I just need some medicine. I'll be fine." He guided me to the sofa and helped me lay down gently.

"I'll go get the meds for ya, ok?" he said as he covered me with a blanket.

I made a small sound to acknowledge him and waited for him to come back with medicine and a drink. After taking the medicine, I just closed my eyes and laid there, willing my body to not betray me like this. Dustin leaned down and kissed me gently on the forehead, causing me to smile slightly.

"Want me to leave ya alone so you can sleep?

"Sleep? Who needs sleep?"

He chuckled. "Ok, why not pop in one of those anime DVDs you like?"

"I just may do that. Would you mind staying down here with me? So I'm not alone?" Times likes these reminded me of being alone after my parents were killed, and despite insisting I could live on my own and take care of myself by the age of ten, I always hated being alone. Then again, could I really say I had ever been alone?

~No, dear hunter. You're never alone. I'm always here with you.~

His voice came across as trying to reassure me. But what was worse? Being alone or having the presence of a vampire in your mind whenever he wanted? *I can't really say if that makes me feel better or not.* I didn't have the energy to fight him off today. I looked at the TV as Dustin popped in a random DVD. After a few minutes of watching in silence, I found myself looking over at him. As he caught me watching him, a small, embarrassed smile came to my lips.

"Medicine helping?"

"Yeah, I think so."

"What's on your mind, sweetheart?"

"Huh? Oh, nothing. Just random thoughts as always." I laughed a nervous sort of laugh. If Dustin knew I had these conversations with Vito, what would he think? Would he feel violated that Vito was in a way in the house with us whenever he wanted?

"You sure?" He raised a single eyebrow at me.

"Yeah, o-of course." *Smile, don't let him know what you're thinking. He'd probably be upset to know that not only does Vito still enter my mind whenever he wants, but that I've started talking back to him.*

~You're right about that.~

"Umm, I'm thinking not. What's wrong? You can tell me."

"It's just that one of the thoughts was about you, that's all."

"Me?" He looks surprised. *If only he knew the full truth.*

~Then tell him. See what happens.~

"Well," I began. *Nope, can't do it. I can't even believe I'm responding to you.* "It's just how you're so good to me, and taking care of me when I don't feel good. And... I love you," I finished lamely.

"That's what I'm here for, love. To make sure you're ok," he smiled. Was he blushing?

"Could you do me one more favor?"

"Sure thing."

"Can I lay on your lap?"

"Umm, ok." He looked a little self-conscious as he scooted over to allow me to lay my head on his lap. Surprisingly, Vito allowed it. Was it because I was sick? Why would that matter to me? "Kel, you still feel really warm. Why don't you just rest today? I'll patrol tonight on my own."

"I'll rest for now. We'll see how I feel tonight and decide." Tonight was our turn on the schedule to patrol, but I didn't like either of us doing vampire patrols on our own. The vampires had been ganging up more and more, which made solo hunting extremely dangerous. We continued to watch TV for a few hours, until Dustin got up to get ready for patrol.

"I feel better now. No more fever. I can go with you."

"Yeah, no more fever 'cause of the medicine. You're staying home tonight, sweetheart. I'll be fine."

"Be careful out there?" I knew there was no use in fighting him. He was easily as stubborn as me, and I knew he was right. The only reason I was feeling better at this moment was because of the medicine. What good would I be on patrol when the medicine wore off? None. I'd turn into a liability, and we couldn't afford that.

"Don't worry, I will be," he chuckled. "Believe me, I don't think anyone wants to mess with me tonight."

I smiled. He's always so confident – maybe too confident. "Should I even ask why they won't wanna mess with you?"

"Cause I'm tired, hungry, and in pain," he grinned.

"Why don't you at least eat something before you go?"

"Sure thing," he grabbed a breakfast bar and held it up as if he had just shot a duck out of midair.

"Dustin, I'm worried about you."

"I'll be fine, sweetie. Promise. Look, if it makes you feel better, I'll only do a few sectors tonight, and I won't do the big ones."

"Thank you. But I still worry you might be a tad crazy."

He gave me a reassuring smile. "I shouldn't be gone for more than an hour and a half or so. Gonna take the motorcycle so it goes quick. See ya!" He closed the door behind him, and moments later I heard the motorcycle roar to life and take off. I went back to watching TV for a bit before dozing off.

I woke with a start and looked at the clock. Three hours had passed since Dustin left. I got up and checked upstairs to see if he had come home while I slept, but the house was empty and quiet. I called his cell phone, but it went to voicemail. *I don't like this. Something doesn't feel right.*

I got dressed in some casual clothes and geared up. Going downstairs to grab the keys to the car, I realized Dustin must've had them when he left. *No big deal, the sectors he went to patrol are close ones tonight.* I grabbed the spare house key and locked up the house before going out to find my partner. As I approached the cemetery, I got chills up my spine.

"Dustin? Where are you?"

"Why not ask Count Vito, sweetie pie?" A voice came from the shadows. It wasn't one I recognized, but I got the immediate feeling I wasn't about to have a pleasant conversation with another living human being. I immediately reached for the dagger I kept at my hip.

"Who said that?"

"Oh, just your ordinary guy, trying to make a buck in this world," the vampire stepped out from the shadows with a smirk that showed one of his fangs.

I turned to walk away and continue my search. I didn't have a lot of extra energy to spend on this guy, and in my haste I didn't take more medicine for my fever, which I was definitely still fighting. He was obviously a lackey vampire, but his mention of Count Vito worried me a bit. He jumped high in the air and landed in front of me, blocking my way as I took a defensive position.

"And where are you going?" he asked coyly. "Now, I'm not here to mess with you, just to deliver a message and then I will be on my way. I can tell you don't trust me."

"Making a buck by being a messenger, huh? Fine, what's the message?" He placed a cell phone with a note attached to it in my hand. I immediately recognized it as Dustin's phone. I opened the note to see what was inside.

Come to the castle. Alone. I have Dustin.
If you want him to live, you will do as I command.

-Vito-

This is my fault. I knew I should've gone with him. Vito knew I wasn't feeling well today. He probably knew Dustin would go patrol alone. Please let him be ok. The castle was only a 30 minute brisk walk from the cemetery. I jogged a bit, but also knew not to tire myself out – I was likely in for a fight of some sort upon arrival. *This is it. I need to be ready to fight Vito, with no hesitations. Dustin's in trouble, and it's my fault. I have to fix this.*

As I approached the cold, wrought iron gates to the castle, I took a steadying breath and focused to get my mental defenses in place. They opened with a soft creak, and I slowly made my way forward. The castle doors opened as I walked up to them, as if of their own accord. Taking another deep breath, I walked in through the enormous wooden doors, which slammed shut behind me. I was locked in.

I'm a vampire hunter, I can do this. Dustin has always been there when I needed him, now it's my turn. I CAN do this. I can face him.

"You look frightened, hunter," Vito's voice was smooth and calm as he appeared in front of me. "Are you afraid?" I glared at his smirking face.

"No, I'm not afraid. Definitely not of you."

"That's fine, you don't need to be afraid of me. But her on the other hand…" He pointed to a shape standing in the shadows behind me. As I slowly turned to look into the shadows, I heard the cool feminine voice ring out.

"Hello there, my *darling*." Her voice was dripping in sarcasm on the last word, as if making fun of the fact that Vito always called me his "darling hunter."

"Claudia." My eye twitched as I realized I would indeed be fighting tonight. I may have hesitations with Vito, but I was ready to sink my claws into this woman, fever or not.

"Remember our deal."

She smiled and gave a slight bow. "Yes, of course."

I couldn't tell if she was responding to me or Vito at that point. There was a cocky look in her eyes when she bowed, staring directly at me. What sort of deal did they make?

"Vito, you can't even scare me, so how do you expect *her* to scare me? Ha! What a joke."

Her eyes narrowed as she took a small step towards me. "Do not underestimate me, little girl."

"Let's see what you've got then, hm?" I drew the blade at my hip and readied myself for battle. Claudia drew a blade of her own and rushed toward me, the look on her face telling me her intention was nothing short of murder. I blocked her swing and pushed her backwards as I started toward her.

Unfortunately, she regained her balance quickly and charged at me again. I stumbled a bit, feeling a little dizzy, but the stumble actually helped me avoid the blade. My chest heaved as we continued, the sound of swords clanging filling the giant room of the castle. I knew I had to take her down quick, before she decided to start throwing me around with magic again. I could feel my fever getting worse as the sweat began to pour from my face.

Magic. Why hasn't she used her magic on me yet? As our swords clashed, a few times it looked like she went to make a gesture, as if to use magic, then thought better of it. *This won't last much longer. I won't make it much longer.*

I lunged at Claudia again, bringing my sword behind me for an overhead blow. However, I didn't follow through with my swing, as she snapped her fingers and laughed. My sword grew heavy as I slowed and fell to the floor. I felt my eyelids grow heavy as I realized she had cast a sleeping spell on me. How could I have forgotten for a single moment that I wasn't just fighting Dustin's ex, but a witch? And magic is so much stronger on a victim when they're sick. How many times did Dustin remind me not to fight blind with rage? To focus? That I shouldn't let my emotions get in the way of a fight? But now, emotions had gotten the better of me, and I was going to pay for it with my life.

Chapter 15

I slowly opened my eyes. Everything was bleary and my head was pounding. *Where am I? What happened?*

"You're safe, hunter. In your chambers, here at my castle."

Right. I was fighting with Claudia, and she magicked me. She didn't kill me, though. Instead, she used a sleeping spell, when I was...

"Dustin. Where is he?" I sat up quickly, as the remnants of the spell washed away and I remembered the events leading up to the fight. My head spun and I had to put a hand on the bed to steady myself. I dimly noted that at least I didn't feel feverish anymore.

"That's not something you need to concern yourself with," Vito replied.

"Yes, it is. He's my... partner," I finished lamely. What could I say? He's my boyfriend? That would spell instant death for him. Even though I knew Count Vito already knew, I just felt that my admitting it to him was probably the worst possible thing.

"Yes, that he is," his mouth twitched into a frown. "Rest, my dear. I have some matters to attend to."

As he walked out of the room, I forced myself to once again get my mental defenses in place. *He said that Dustin is my partner, not was. That means Dustin's alive, and he's probably here somewhere. I need to find him, to get him out of here.*

I waited a couple of minutes to make sure the Count wasn't going to come right back in, then got out of bed and put my shoes back on. Peeking my head through the door, I noticed there were less vampires roaming around than the last time I was here. I caught a glimpse of Vito as he exited through the large front doors, a resounding thud as they closed behind him.

I exited my room and went down the grand staircase. *If I were a vampire, where would I keep my prisoners? Probably an old dungeon.* Moving slowly and cautiously, I wandered the bottom floor, peeking into every door, looking for a dungeon. Finally, one door led to a staircase going down. I picked my way down the stairs into a dimly lit room – an actual, old fashioned dungeon. *Does he really have to follow the clichés?*

I paused as I entered the room, preparing myself for a possible battle. Upon looking around, I heard a soft breathing and saw a figure, hands shackled and hung by chains.

"Dustin?" I was afraid I may have just walked into a trap set by the Count. I couldn't afford to rush in if this person were anyone other than Dustin. If he had indeed laid out a trap for me and I fell into it, what would Vito do to Dustin when he found out?

"K…Kel…" His voice was a hoarse whisper. I ran over to Dustin, who looked half alive, and lightly hugged him as he groaned in pain.

"What happened?" I asked as I started fiddling with the shackles, hoping for some easy and quick way to open them.

"You don't wanna know. Kel! Behind you!"

As I quickly turned around, I noticed two vampire goons headed my way. Of course Vito must have had a patrol keeping an eye on Dustin. "Son of a biscuit!" As I began the battle with the patrols, I noticed another figure moving in the shadows. I heard a thud as I finished up my battle, then raced over to Dustin, who now laid in an unmoving heap on the floor. I looked around to see who set him free, but saw no one.

~Take Dustin and run, Kel. Don't ask why. I just couldn't see it end for him like that. Quickly. The Count will be back soon.~

For the first time ever, the voice inside my head wasn't the voice of Vito, but Claudia. I heard the great door above close and knew I had no escape.

~No time.~

From the shadows, Claudia snapped her fingers and Dustin and I were surrounded by smoke. When the smoke cleared, I stood in my living room with Dustin at my feet. I dragged Dustin to the sofa and laid him on it before going to grab a bowl of warm water and a cloth to wipe his wounds clean.

"What was that all about? I can't under why Claudia would do that, when she's been trying so hard to help Vito out," I wondered aloud. As I wiped the blood from Dustin's face, I noticed a slight mark on his cheek – the form of lips. Lipstick. I wiped away the tears that began stinging in my eyes. "She loves him," I whispered. *Is that why she was helping Vito? To get me out of the way so she can have Dustin back for herself? If so, it's a twisted sort of love.*

I felt a slight movement and looked down as Dustin began to stir. "How are you feeling?"

"Could be better," he tried to chuckle.

"Shh, you're hurt."

"What happened? The last thing I remember is being jumped in the cemetery and the rest is fuzzy."

I took a deep breath. This wasn't going to be pleasant. "Vito captured you. He told me to come to the castle alone, and then… Claudia was there. I tried to fight her, but she cast a sleeping spell on me. The next thing I knew, I was waking up in a bed with Vito watching over me. When he stepped out, I went looking for you. When I got down to the dungeon, two of Vito's goons came up behind me and attacked me. While I was fighting them off," my breath caught. "Someone else set you free."

"Someone else?"

I paused for a moment. He wasn't in good shape, and I knew the news would be shocking. But I had to tell him. "Claudia set you free, and then told me to hurry up and get you out of there. But Vito came back, so she used her magic to send us here."

"Claudia did what?!?" Dustin grabbed his head, which I could imagine was throbbing both with pain and confusion. I simply nodded.

"The only thing I could think of is… she loves you." I held up a small mirror that decorated the table so he could see the lipstick mark on his cheek.

"N… no, I don't think so. That's a part of my life that died. For her too, I'm sure." He took a shaky breath.

"I wouldn't be too sure about that, Dustin." What was the feeling in my stomach right now? Jealousy? Pity?

"Oh yeah, I'm sure of it," he said as he wiped the lipstick away. "I'm sure it was just another one of her games. I don't know where you came up with that idea, but Claudia was probably playing games with you and I to get us second guessing our actions and to try to freak us out."

"I don't know, maybe," I sighed. "Now hold still so I can wash up the rest of the blood." I needed something to distract myself from the conversation.

"Do you happen to know where my phone is?"

"Yeah, hang on," I wiped a bit more blood from his arm, then grabbed his phone from my back pocket and handed it to him before going back to cleaning his wounds. Dustin pressed a few buttons and seemed to be reading something when his eyes went wide.

"I get a feeling that face wasn't in response to your wounds," I said.

"A text message."

"What was it?"

"143434."

"What's that supposed to mean?"

"I have no idea. I don't even recognize the number it came from." Despite his words, I had a nagging feeling that he knew exactly what it was and just wasn't telling me. "You ok?" He looked at me with a mixture of pain and concern.

"Yeah, I'll be ok," I nodded. He slowly placed his hand on my arm. I could tell every movement was difficult for him right now.

"I love you."

"I love you, too."

"Thanks for coming to get me."

"Of course. That's what we do. We're partners." I smiled at him. "Now rest."

He smiled back at me and relaxed his head into the pillow on the sofa, closed his eyes, and drifted off to sleep. I cleaned up the rags and bowl of water, then sank into the chair by the sofa. I closed my eyes and tried to block out the racing thoughts.

Why did Vito beat Dustin, but not kill him? What's his goal? And Claudia... why did she help us? What kind of game is she playing? Am I right? Does she love him? Is she just trying to get back to Dustin? To get me out of the way?

~Calm your thoughts, hunter. All will be revealed in due time.~
What do you want?

~Right now? Peace and quiet. However, I cannot ignore your racing mind.~

I thought you had to choose to listen to my mind? What are you up to?

~Usually, yes. However, we share a connection, my dear hunter. There are times your thoughts travel to me without any effort on my part.~

What games are you playing? What's going to be revealed?

~In due time, hunter. In due time. Now rest.~

My eyes grew heavy. I couldn't be sure if it was the stress of the day, or Vito and his influence on me. The next thing I knew, the sun was shining through the windows. I didn't remember falling asleep, and had no dreams. I rose to check on Dustin and noticed a paper crumpled on the floor.

Dustin,

By the time you read this note, you will hopefully be safe. I know you won't understand my actions. I'm not sure I even understand them. However, I still love you. I realize now I grew to love you back then, and I probably always will. I'm so sorry.

Claudia

I shook as I finished reading the note. *I was right.* I dropped the note back onto the floor and went to the kitchen. *Cook breakfast. It'll be a good distraction.* Dustin woke as I finished the waffles and bacon. I poured us each a glass of orange juice, then helped him to the table.

"How are you feeling?"

"Like I got hit by a truck. Or beaten to a pulp by a vampire."

"Gee, I wonder why," I chuckled. "Um, Dustin? I picked up a piece of paper from the floor this morning. I thought it was the note I had got from Vito. I wasn't snooping or anything."

"It's ok. I thought I threw it in the trash. I guess I missed a bit to the left, huh?"

"Yeah."

"Umm... I take it you read it?"

"Yeah," I looked down at my waffle. "I'm sorry. I didn't mean to be nosy or anything like that."

"Kel… It's ok. In the note, as you read, it explains why she helped you free me and how she still has some feelings for me. That definitely came as a shock to me, figuring she left me saying she hated me. I, however, do not share the same feelings about her. She ripped my heart out and stomped on it a few times before leaving. I am grateful that she helped you rescue me, but that can't repair the heartache she caused."

I nodded as he spoke. "I know, it's just… weird to think about, I guess. I mean, why would she be helping Vito, who's trying to kill you, if she loves you?"

"I don't know. Maybe at the time she wanted to get back at me. Or maybe… Nah, never mind, that's absurd." He shoved a bite of waffle in his mouth and looked away.

"What?"

"Maybe she's trying to get rid," he swallowed the waffle and continued, "to get rid of you?"

I closed my eyes and sighed. "That's what I was thinking last night."

He shook his head, as if trying to deny the fact that what he suggested was even plausible.

"Well, we won't know until we ask her, will we?" I finished the last bite of my waffle. "But first thing's first… you have to give your body time to heal."

"I always do. Well, sorta." He smirked.

"Heh, yeah, sorta." I laughed. He raised an eyebrow at me.

"Not like you do, either."

"Who, me?" I put on my best innocent face as he managed a slight laugh. "Alright, enough chit chat. I'm going down to the basement to train a bit." I stood and cleared my dishes.

"Yeah, I'm gonna go try to take a shower."

"Just don't slip and fall. That's the last thing we need right now."

Another chuckle. "Yeah, I bet."

* * * * *

Down in the gym, I set my bottle of water on the table, turned on some upbeat music, and began some warm up stretches. Once I felt warmed up, I went straight for the punching bag and just let all of my emotions out on it. After several minutes, I noticed the bag starting to come apart. It was old anyway, but I didn't want to deal with it, so I moved on to the dummies to practice some of my kicks. Finally feeling as though I had exerted most of my emotions through physical activity, I dropped to the floor and lay there for several minutes. Eventually, with a heavy sigh, I rose from the floor to go back upstairs.

On my way to shower, I peeked into Dustin's room. He lay sprawled on his bed, freshly showered.

"Hey you."

He turned his head to look over at me. "Hey."

"How ya feeling?"

"Crappy," he replied with a groan.

"I'm sorry," I sat in a chair next to his bed and rested my chin in my hands on the bed next to his pillow. "Anything I can do to help?"

"Yeah, on that hook over there is my gun belt. You wanna just put a bullet in my head that would be awesome." He tried to laugh at his own sarcastic joke but caught his breath from the pain it caused.

I rolled my eyes at him. "Can't be too bad if you can still be sarcastic. If you can think of anything I can actually help with, let me know, ok?"

He nodded. "Ok, sounds good."

I gave him a gentle hug, then stood up. "Get some rest, ok? I'm gonna shower, then go shopping. We're pretty much out of food."

"Ok, I'll try. One thing before you go, though?"

"Hmm?"

He beckoned me closer with his finger. I leaned down and he kissed me softly on the lips. "You can go under one condition. You must buy chocolate milk and mint chocolate chip ice cream. The green kind." He grinned and I smiled.

"Ok, I will." I walked out of his room and went to take a quick shower. Afterwards, I went downstairs to prepare myself. *I can't let him know I'm going back to the Count's castle. I know I'm being stupid, but I need some answers.* I wrote a note to Dustin detailing where I was really going, and left it by the door, just in case things went south. I grabbed the car keys and slowly stepped outside, preparing myself for both a fight and answers I may not actually want to hear.

As I approached the large iron gates once again, I looked back to the car, wondering if I was doing the right thing. I took a deep breath as I pushed the iron gates open and walked up to the large front doors. After a quick knock, the heavy doors opened, admitting me into the great marbled hall on the bottom floor of the castle. I looked up to the second floor balcony and saw Count Vito standing there, watching me as I stepped inside.

"I knew you'd be back, my dear."

"Sorry, I'm not here to see you. I need to talk to Claudia." I'm sure my voice was dripping with attitude, but I hadn't prepared myself for a fight with Vito. I had questions for Claudia, and I wanted answers.

"Dah, very well," he said with a shrug of his bare shoulders. He took a sip from his wine glass and knocked on a door before returning to the banister to gaze down at me again. Moments later, Claudia appeared, tying a robe around her waist.

"What is it, hunter? As you can see, I'm not in the mood for visitors."

"I'm not here to fight. I need to talk to you. Alone." I looked at Vito. He smirked and walked into another room – I imagined his bedchamber, as he would call it – as Claudia walked down the staircase, each step padding as soft as a cat. I spoke in a low voice as soon as she stepped off the bottom stair. I wasn't sure exactly how much Vito knew.

"Why did you set Dustin free? I thought you were helping Vito."

She sighed. "I don't know, Kel. I saw Dustin hanging there half alive, and… I just couldn't stand to see him get tortured like that. You weren't here when Vito's lackeys tortured him. I could hear his screams from all the way up there." She pointed to the room she had come out of.

"Vito had left, so they gave Dustin everything they could."

"So… pretty much, you set him free because of guilt?"

"A little," she looked away and down to the floor. "Look, don't think I'm turning good or anything. That was a one shot deal."

"Noted. However, I seem to remember one of our encounters, you told me Vito wanted nothing with me," *which I know isn't true,* "so why did he tell me to come alone for Dustin?"

She shrugged. "I'm not the one who hasn't had someone in my bed in 100 years. Ask him?" She eyeballed me for a moment then. "He is very fond of you, you know that, right? Of course, I can't quite blame him. You are rather attractive."

"Still… I've been hunting him. Trying to kill him. It makes no sense. But that's not what I came here for. Are you sure you didn't set Dustin free because you still have feelings for him?" Her eyes narrowed. "I'm right, aren't I?"

"I… no! I have no feelings for him anymore."

"I read your note. And had already figured out your feelings before that. But… if you do have feelings for him, then why have you been helping Vito, who wants to kill him?"

"I – because I found that my powers were needed with the dark side. And I was very vindictive towards Dustin." She snapped her head away from me, averting my gaze. "Look, we all have fears and we all make bad decisions. I just can't back out of this one."

"Why can't you? I don't understand. Did you sell your soul or something to Vito?"

"Something like that." She looked back at me. "What Dustin probably told you is true. I died. Vito brought me back. Cared for me when I was weak."

"So he brought you back because…?"

"I'm not sure if he knew I was a witch before bringing me back or not. It's not like he tells me everything. But we made a blood pact. I have to help him now."

"But you have feelings for Dustin."

"I have feelings for both. Ok, there, I said it. I know I can't have Dustin. I do love him, but I also love Vito for healing me and caring for me. Nurturing me back to health. Go ahead and say it. I'm a confused, sorry little girl."

"No. You do love them both, just in different ways. I know that feeling."

"I'm sure." She rolled her eyes as if I were placating her. She had no idea just how much I understood her having feelings for both Dustin and Vito.

"No woman is a stranger to that feeling, Claudia."

"Perhaps," she said with a shrug. "Look, Kel. You're treating me like another person, which is more than most do for me. And I actually am starting to like you a bit. Maybe even a lot. But I have to play for the other team."

"The other team… Vito? So capture me or die trying? Is that it?"

"Naïve girl," she scoffed. "The Count can have you whenever he decides he's ready. This was merely an opportunity to avoid long term servitude. Either way, I can't change my allegiance. I will do what he wishes, or I will die. That's part of our pact. I have no choice." A single tear made its way down her cheek. "I'm sorry. I didn't know you at the time I made the pact. You were a name without a face. And someone I wanted out of my way."

I didn't know what I had really been expecting, but it wasn't this. Maybe a bit of a fight with an evil woman with no heart, but not a conversation with a woman who felt just as deeply confused as I did. I had no idea what to say, so I stood there quietly.

"You have given me a lot to think about tonight. I'm sorry for still loving Dustin. Maybe it'll go away after a while. I'm just glad he has someone like you now. However," she rose her chin in an almost proud fashion, "the next time we meet, we will still be enemies. Don't expect another chat like today."

"You can't help who you love, Claudia. I wish you well. Until we meet again." I turned and walked out the great front doors, pausing at the thud behind me. My heart pounded in my chest.

Love. She loves them both. I do understand that. I love Dustin. And I think in a way, I love Vito. Maybe not the same kind of love, but some kind of love.

Chapter 16

I walked in the front door and put away the chocolate milk and ice cream Dustin had asked for. I checked the table – the note was still there. Grabbing it, I tore it to pieces and threw it away. I made my way up quietly to Dustin's room.

"You awake?" I peeked my head through his door.

"Hey, yeah, I'm awake," he replied groggily. "I must've fallen asleep."

Good. He doesn't know.

"Thanks for being understanding earlier. About the whole Claudia thing. I know things have gotten tough lately. I'm just glad that you're still by my side." He smiled.

"Hey, no prob. I'll always be here for you," I smiled back briefly before staring out of the window. *"The Count can have you whenever he decides he's ready," Claudia said. Is that true? If it is… I can't always be there for Dustin.*

"As will I for you," he reached over and grabbed my hand. "I'll make sure that Vito or Claudia don't do anything bad to you."

"Yeah, I'm not so sure Claudia's really all that bad…" I bit my lip, realizing what I said after the words escaped my mouth. I looked back at Dustin to see his mouth agape, pure shock on his face.

"Umm, hello? She was trying to kill you to get to me!"

"She loves you, she just doesn't how to let you know. But it doesn't matter," I shook my head.

"You're right, it doesn't matter. She can love me all she wants. But she ain't getting me," he smirked. "Just be glad that she wants me and not you. I'd hate to see how that would turn up. She's kind of intense."

I felt my eye twitch as I remembered Claudia stating that she could see why Vito was fond of me and that I was attractive.

"That she is." I stood up, feeling the need to be alone with my thoughts. "You get some more rest. Your body's been through a lot."

He laid back down as I headed downstairs to play some video games. I popped in a fighting game. Something that was somewhat mindless that I could play and still let my thoughts roam.

Was she right? Does Vito find me attractive as well? Is that why he goes on about protecting me and my innocence? No, there has to be something more to it. I've never been able to figure this out. Why does he toy with me? Play those games of his? What's his goal?

~143434.~

I quickly paused my game. *What?*

~The answers to your questions lie within that. I believe you're ready to learn about it, dear hunter.~

And what is it?

~Dah, you can figure that one out, if you think you're truly ready for answers.~

Tell me it again. I want answers. And this better not be a trap.

~143434.~

I scribbled the numbers down on a piece of paper. *Why does that number sound familiar? I feel like I've heard it before.*

No answer. Agitated, I continued my game. I felt a lot like the characters right now – being beat up and played with as if what I wanted didn't matter. I continued my digital onslaught until I fell asleep on the sofa.

I woke the next morning full of resolve. Looking at the paper with the numbers on it, I decided to hop right on the computer and start searching. After an hour or so with no results, I went upstairs to check in on Dustin. He watched as I opened his door and stepped in.

"Hey you. You're up early," he smiled.

"You, too. How ya feeling this morning?"

"Still sore, but a little better."

"Breakfast?"

"Scrambled eggs?"

"Sure."

I nodded and went back downstairs to cook. It had been a restless night, and my mind felt as scrambled as the eggs I was now cooking. *143434. Where have I heard that? Why can't I remember?*

I took a plate of eggs and a glass of orange juice up to Dustin. I sat in the chair while he ate, lost in my thoughts.

"You ok?" Dustin asked between bites.

"Hm? Yeah, why?"

"You're quiet."

"Oh. Yeah, I just didn't sleep well, so I'm still kinda tired."

He took a sip of juice and just stared at me. He knew I wasn't being entirely honest, of course. Even tired, I was usually more talkative than this. But those numbers that Vito had told me were stuck in my head.

"Could you hand me my notebook, Kel?" I snapped my attention back to him. I looked around to the desk in his room and saw his notebook sitting there.

"Yeah, sure," I said, grabbing the notebook and handing it to him. "You all done with breakfast?"

"Yeah, thank you."

"Ok, I'm going to go clean up and see what news I can find online. You get some more rest today, got it? You still look drained."

"You got it. I'm just gonna sit here and go through some notes."

"Mm-hmm," I said as I walked out of his room and headed downstairs to clean up from breakfast. I grabbed myself a glass of orange juice and sat back at the computer to continue my search. Nothing yielded results. Basic searches returned a bunch of random phone numbers. Vampire hunter forums had absolutely nothing. I even searched through old emails. Not a single crumb.

Are you listening?

Silence. Something told me, however, that he was present and listening. Almost like I could feel his hand laying on my shoulder, him standing behind me. It felt so real I had to turn my head quickly just to make sure he wasn't actually there.

Can't you give me something more to go on? Some sort of direction?

More silence. Whatever these numbers were, Count Vito obviously meant it when he said that if I wanted answers, I would figure it out. After a full day of fruitless searching online, I fell asleep sitting at the computer.

The next morning, I decided to head to the next town over, where the Vampire Hunter Academy was located. It made sense – Vito was a vampire, and he was the one to give me the numbers. Maybe something in the library there would be helpful. Or maybe someone there knew something about these mysterious numbers. I made a couple of quick peanut butter and jelly sandwiches for breakfast and took one up to Dustin, who raised an eyebrow at me when I set down the sandwich on his nightstand.

"I want to go to VHA. Maybe find some new resources for our fight against Claudia and Vito."

"Mm." He took a bite of his sandwich. I knew he was suspicious, but the need to figure out these numbers was eating away at me. Somehow, I knew the numbers were important, and that Vito was telling the truth when he told me that my questions would be answered when I discovered what these numbers meant. My entire being was burning for answers.

"I'll be back a bit later. Don't do anything crazy while I'm gone."

"Figured on doing some training today."

"Light training?"

"Yeah, I won't push it too much."

"Ok," I nodded. "Nothing too crazy." I smiled and gave him a quick kiss on the cheek.

"And you be safe. Vampire attacks have been on the rise, and who knows what Claudia and Vito are planning. As if Vito didn't have it in for us enough already, add in a crazy ex and it's impossible to get a break now."

"Yeah," I grinned. "Alright, be back later." I made my way to my bedroom to put on some fresh clothes. As I entered, I shuddered. Memories of childhood flooded by mind again.

"-legacy family, you imbecile."

"How was I meant to know? They were kept secret."

"You almost ruined everything." A dangerously low voice that let the other person know they were in big trouble.

I shook my head back to the present. *What was that? Felt like a memory, but I've never remembered it before.* I quickly changed and got my boots on. I made my way to the Academy, my heart racing at what I imagined was a memory.

In the Academy library, I searched for vampire lore, history, even looking through listings of vampires, both past and present. Nothing. I searched for a call number on the spine of a book, thinking maybe it was referencing a certain book.

"Nothing," I growled. I finally turned to a librarian for help.

"143434? Hmm, I don't recall it in any of the books I've gone through," he said.

"Wait a minute," said a voice behind him. "Wasn't there a group of students who were doing research awhile back with their research project numbered 143434?"

"Oh, probably, yeah," the librarian replied. He rustled through some papers until he found what he was looking for. "Here we go. Let's see, research projects starting with 1 denote the history department, and 43 falls under Professor Carroway. Here's his office number. You can ask him if he still has the project info."

"Thanks," I said, taking the slip of paper and heading out of the library. As I approached the office door, I saw it was open. A student was walking out as I came to the door, almost running right into me. Professor Carroway stood behind him. I vaguely recognized him, although I hadn't taken any classes with him. He was around his mid-fifties, with graying hair and an ever present smile that depicted his jovial personality perfectly.

"Good afternoon, Professor Carroway?"

"Yes, how can I help you?"

"I wanted to ask you a question about a research project."

"Of course, of course. Come on in. Which class are you in my dear?"

"I'm not, actually. But some information I came across led me here, and I think it might be related to an old research project some of your students conducted."

"Ah, ok then. Do you have the project number?"

"143434."

His eyes widened briefly before regaining his composure. He turned to a filing cabinet against the wall.

"Yes, I remember that one rather well. Let's see if I can find it for you. What sort of information led you to this particular project?"

"A vampire."

"I gathered it was related to a vampire. I was merely curious, child." His tone sounded amused.

Can I trust him? And what if I'm wrong and it has nothing to do with the research project? Then I'd just be wasting my time and his. And what do I tell him? That Count Vito spoke the numbers in my mind and told me to figure them out? Even I'm starting to think I really am going crazy right now.

"It had to do with a hunting party that was going after an elite vampire. I didn't catch the name," I lied.

"I see. Here we are," he pulled a file folder out of the drawer. "It was a rather interesting project. Some of my top students that year," he chuckled as he handed me the folder. I accepted the folder from him and opened it to see the cover page of a research paper.

Research Project #143434
The Secret to Elite Vampire Longevity
By: Abbot, Sherry; Lewis, Anthony; Sheen, Dustin

I heard myself gasp as I read his name. *Dustin? How could he be related to this?* I ran through the numbers in my mind again and remembered now the night we got back from the count's castle. He had received a text message and read the number out loud: 143434. But he had said that he had no idea what it meant, and it was a wrong number.

~He lied.~

Is this what I was supposed to find?

~Yes, dear hunter. Read on.~

I had a feeling I didn't want to stand here and read this with an audience. The feeling I had in my stomach told me I needed solitude for this.

"Umm, Professor? Would it be possible for me to get a copy of this paper? I'd love the chance to read it over, but would hate to take up your valuable time." I flashed him a winsome smile.

"Absolutely. Let me go make a copy for you. Wait here."

"Thank you." I stood waiting in his office as he walked out to make my copy. Those few minutes I had to wait felt like an eternity, and when he handed me the papers, it took all my effort to walk away and not run. I was finally about to get some answers to the questions that had been burning for years. But how did Dustin play a role in all of this? I exited the building and looked around. Finding a tree to offer shade, I went and sat under it to begin reading.

Research Project #143434
The Secret to Elite Vampire Longevity
By: Abbot, Sherry; Lewis, Anthony; Sheen, Dustin

Vampire lore has long spoken of elite vampires, however humans have never been able to extract much information regarding them. How did they come to be? What makes them elite? What gives them power over other vampires? These are the sorts of questions we set out to answer.

Pouring over history books led us to tracing the history of a few select elite vampires: Lydia, Lafayette, and Vito. These were the only three elite vampires for whom history documented the approximate year they became referred to as elite, which was the same year when there was also documentation for what passes as marriage in the vampire world. It would appear that the "elite" status was bestowed upon each of these vampires upon their first marital pairing. Although uncommon for a vampire to take a human spouse, it is not altogether unheard of. However, the simple act of taking a human spouse does not seem to be sufficient to achieve the "elite" status.

In order to understand why these pairings were special, it seemed imperative to understand if there was something different in these pairings from the other pairings that did not elevate a vampire to "elite" status. Indeed, the families that each spouse came from were old families that had a long standing history with vampires. Each of the families had described a run in with vampires that did not result in their loss of life.

We then set out to conduct interviews with vampires in order to gain some insider information. Although these low level vampires did not have much information, several mentioned a vampire history book that speaks of elite vampires and legacy families. None of the interviewed vampires could offer any specific information on what these legacy families were, however each one noted that they were important in order for a vampire to achieve and retain "elite" status, each offering different pieces to the puzzle.

This paper takes a deeper look into the families that each spouse of an "elite" vampire came from, and works to determine what makes these families different. Why are these specific families targeted by vampires as spouses instead of meals?

The summary alone had my heart racing. There was so much information to take in, I actually had to read it twice to make sure I didn't misunderstand anything. A vampire needed to take a spouse from what was considered a legacy family in order to achieve elite status? How did this even make any sense? I began to pour over the pages of research and notes.

Legacy families were evidently old families that had some special properties to their blood, allowing them to resist being turned into a vampire, but only so long as they didn't have too much blood drained. If a vampire drank the blood of one of these legacy family members, it allowed them to hone skills that normal vampires couldn't tap into. Vampires who came across these legacy families began taking a spouse in order to continue having the blood available for longer periods of time. However, they could never turn the spouse into a vampire, or the blood would lose its special properties.

I closed my eyes for a moment as my mind raced. This wasn't something we learned in our hunter training. I wasn't even sure the information was completely accurate, since it was a student research paper. But why would Count Vito point me to it if it weren't relevant?

Wait… why did *he point me to it? Why do I need to be reading this? He said to pursue it if I was ready to learn the answers to my questions.*

~Yes, my dear. These are the answers to the questions that have plagued you for years.~

I jumped. I was so lost in my thoughts that I hadn't expected him to be present on this journey as well. It didn't feel like there was any room in my mind with my own thoughts racing around in there. I looked back down at the papers and pretended to be in deep concentration over them. I didn't need any students walking by to become suspicious of me.

My questions… you mean this is the answer to why I was spared?

~Yes.~

But then that would mean…

~Go ahead.~

Are you telling me I'm from a legacy family?

~Very good.~

But you're already an elite vampire. Why would you need me?

~Continue reading.~

I furrowed my brows as I focused my attention to the pages and continued to read. Because the spouse could not be turned, eventually the blood supply ran out when the spouse finally passed away. The elite vampires noticed that their special skills began to diminish after some time. Eventually, they realized that they needed new blood from a legacy family member every 100 years in order to retain their skills.

Every 100 years? Why did that set off bells in my head? I thought back to my encounters with the Count. Almost a hundred years. Ninety-eight long, cold years of being alone, he had said. *Ninety-eight years of being alone. I'm from a legacy family? You want to make me your bride – not to turn me into a vampire, but to retain your elite status?*

~You are partly correct.~

I wanted to ask him which part was correct, but my cell phone rang and interrupted my thoughts. I quickly grabbed it and looked to see who was calling me during such an important moment. Dustin.

"Hello?" I answered.

"Hey, you been gone awhile. Everything ok?"

"Yeah, just looking into some info here at the Academy still."

"Oh. Having any luck?"

"Yeah, I think so. I'll be back soonish. I'll stop and grab some dinner to bring home."

"Sounds good. I'll see you soon, Kel."

"Yeah, see you soon, Dustin."

Chapter 17

I hesitated at the front door. *How am I going to approach the subject of his research project? How can I tell him I may be from a legacy family? I wouldn't even know where to begin.* I took a deep breath. *Any words of wisdom you want to offer?*

~You're on your own here, hunter. I've led you down the path to the answers you seek. It's up to you now.~

Thanks, I thought sarcastically. Another deep breath. *Here I go.* I opened the door and stepped inside, looking around. Dustin sat on the sofa, playing a fighting game. He turned his head at the sound of the door.

"Hey, you."

"Hey back. I picked up some Italian food for dinner."

"Great, I'm starving!" He paused his game and grinned at the bag of food.

"Let me guess, you didn't eat lunch?"

"Yes I did," he replied, acting offended.

"Peanut butter and jelly sandwich?"

"Macaroni and cheese."

"Figures," I laughed as I made my way to the kitchen table with our food. "Come on out and eat."

He got up from the sofa and grabbed drinks from the refrigerator while I laid out the food. As I inhaled the wonderful aroma of chicken Alfredo, I realized *I* hadn't eaten lunch. I was so engrossed in figuring out what those numbers meant, and then reading the research, that I had lost all track of time. I was ravenous.

The first few minutes of dinner passed in a peaceful quiet. However, as our bellies started to feel a little more satisfied, Dustin felt ready for discussion.

"So, what did you find at the Academy?"

I stopped chewing my food for a moment and looked at him. I finished what was in my mouth as I felt my stomach knot up.

"Well, I didn't have much to go on to start with. But it finally led me to an old research paper."

"Oh really?"

He shoveled another bite of food into his mouth as he looked at me curiously. I took another slow bite of food to avoid having to answer. I wasn't sure if I was ready for this conversation yet. For the information he might have. *What else might he know about legacy families? Did he know when we got partnered up that I'm from a legacy family?*

"So? Are you gonna tell me what you found out or not?"

"Well," I began. "I think you may actually know more about it than I do."

"Really?" He looked confused. "Why's that? Was it research from one of my old professors or something?"

"143434."

He froze and his eyes widened. Slowly, he set down his fork and finished the bite of food in his mouth. "Where did you come across that?" he asked.

"In the castle," I lied. I still wasn't ready to tell him about the conversations between Vito and I that took place in my head. They felt somehow intimate. "Back when Vito had captured you. I saw the numbers written on a piece of paper and thought they might be important."

"I see," he nodded. After a moment, he sighed and continued. "Well, what could I tell you that you didn't already read about in the paper?"

"What else do you know about legacy families?"

"Not much. We couldn't get a lot of information on them. Mostly what we found was legends and rumors. What we did find is there was enough evidence to safely assume the existence of legacy families. We spoke to one vampire that corroborated that as

140

well. He said there's a history book that talks about them, but it's rare and only in the library of a few vampires. No regular human has access to them."

"Do you know where the legacy families are?"

"No. We couldn't confirm locations for the few families we could find info on. What's this about?"

Do I tell him? It doesn't sound like he knew. But am I really from a legacy family? What would that do to us? Our relationship? Claudia said Vito could lay claim on me whenever he chooses. Does that mean I have no choice in my fate?

~You have a choice, my dear. Maybe not the choices you are contemplating, but you do have a choice.~

"I have some more research to do to confirm some stuff, but I think the legacy family stuff may be related to our hunt."

"Yeah, well, Vito's an elite vampire, so definitely a relationship there."

"Why didn't you ever tell me about this before?"

"It never really came up. And a lot of what we had to work on to start with was speculation. Plus we were going on the word of a vampire. We went with it, but you still have to wonder how much we could trust him."

"Yeah, I guess so." I went back to taking small bites of my food.

"What's up, Kel? You seem really bothered by this."

"Did you ever find information on any legacy families around here?"

"One, from almost a century ago."

"Where are they now?"

"Dunno. They disappeared. No record of them. Never found records of death for the last generation, and I guess they had no kids." He watched me intently as I mulled over my thoughts.

That must've been my family. Did they go into hiding to evade the vampires wanting to become elite? Were my parents trying to hide me?

"You said there's a history book that talks about them? Any idea where the closest one is?"

"Can't be sure, but it's likely there's one in Count Vito's castle, since he's an elite. He probably had to get some information before tracking down the right family."

~Well, it seems your partner is not a complete idiot.~

You have the book? I nodded, as if contemplating Dustin's words.

~Dah.~

I want to see it.

~As you wish, my dear. Shall I pop in with it now?~ I could almost hear his smile as he spoke in my mind.

Of course not. You know Dustin doesn't know about these… conversations.

~Then you plan to walk back into the den of the Count once more?~ He chuckled.

You won't hurt me. I was confident of that now.

~You are correct, my dear.~

"He has the book. Without a doubt. I'm going tomorrow morning."

"What?! Kel, what are you thinking?"

"I need that book. I can get it."

"Yeah, but can you come back out alive if you go alone? I don't think so. I'm going with you."

"No, I can do this. It's something I have to do myself."

"Kel, what has gotten into you? You're acting really… weird."

"Just trust me on this. Please."

He shoved his last bite of food in his mouth with a scowl on his face. I knew that if I went alone, Vito would allow me to look at the book in question. But if Dustin were there? I doubted things would go very smoothly.

"Fine. But I don't like this. And if you're not back by 5:00, I'm coming after you."

"Deal. I'll go right after breakfast."

~And I'll be waiting, dear hunter, with book in hand.~

And Claudia?

~She's gone for a few days.~

Good. I didn't feel like I needed to deal with her on top of what I may be learning tomorrow.

* * * * *

I laid my hand on the cold metal gate and paused. This was it. If that book said everything I thought it might, I may finally have answers as to why I was spared when my parents were killed. Answers to why Count Vito had been protecting me and my "innocence," as he so often put it. Answers as to why I actually felt safe when I could feel him watching me. And maybe answers to why I always hesitated when it came time to fight him.

I thought back to Dustin at breakfast. He was fuming and worried. I can't say I blamed him. If the roles were reversed, I'd probably be feeling the same way. But the roles weren't reversed, and here I was. Once again at the gates to the castle of Count Vito. Drawn back by unknown forces and the desire to know what they were.

I pushed the gate open and walked to the front door. The massive door opened as I approached it. As I entered, I gazed around and noticed Vito sitting in a plush arm chair in a sitting room off to the side of the majestic staircase. As promised, he had a book in hand. As I entered the room, he set down a glass of red wine on the table between the two arm chairs. I noticed a second glass on the table as he motioned for me to sit.

"Welcome back, my dear," he greeted me as I stiffly took my seat in the chair opposite him. He closed the book and held it out to me. "I believe this is what you're here for?"

"You tell me," I responded as I gingerly took the book, noting just how old it felt.

He chuckled. "I believe you'll find exactly what you've been looking for, even if they're not the answers you wanted." He stood and left the room for a few minutes. I caressed the old book in my hand, as if coaxing it to tell me all of its secrets. I looked up as the Count walked back in with another book in hand. Evidently I would have company during this journey of mine.

I opened the cover of the book and gently turned the first few pages when I noticed a bookmark just barely sticking up from the pages. Intrigued, I turned to the page. It was a chapter all about legacy families, and judging by the wear of the book, Vito seemed to have turned to this section several times.

Legacy families are rare, estimated at less than 1% of the population, as there is a genetic mutation in their blood that allows them to have their blood mostly drained without succumbing to the venom that changes them into a vampire. There appears to be a heritable factor, as children of those with the genetic mutation each present with the same mutation. Testing has shown that a vampire who drinks the blood of a legacy patron will have his or her powers enhanced. The amount of time this enhancement lasts is unclear, however may last up to one hundred years after consuming the blood.

To change a legacy member is difficult, but can be done. One must drain just enough blood to weaken the body, without draining too much, thereby leaving the body unable to revive. However, research indicates that when this is completed, the blood loses its properties and no longer enhances the abilities of a vampire.

A vampire who has consumed the mutated blood has come to be known as an "elite" vampire, indicating the superior abilities gained upon consuming the blood of a legacy family member.

I paused and stared off into space. *According to this book, legacy families are real. And according to Vito, I come from a legacy family. Which also means…*

I looked over at Vito, who had raised his head to meet my gaze. "Do continue, my dear," he urged.

"I'm from a legacy family. Which means that if a vampire bites me, I'm not likely to die and become one from a simple bite?"

"Correct."

"And you made sure no vampire ever bit me… to keep this a secret?"

He nodded.

"But it also means I'd be sought after if vampires knew this."

"Also correct."

"Why don't more vampires know?"

"Some are told of legacy families. But a vampire has to be matured enough to handle legacy blood and not be overwhelmed by it, ending up in a frenzy. However your case is a bit different."

"Different how?"

A small smile that had a mixture of relief and regret appeared on his face. Was I imagining it? Did the Count ever actually regret anything?

"There was one legacy family, many years ago, that went into hiding. They did so because a rule had been broken. Normally, a vampire isn't allowed to procreate with a human. The results are often mixed, with the child unable to survive in either human or vampire societies. They are not exactly one of the undead, but often still have the fangs that denote vampires, if the child even survives. This particular legacy family, however, had a member who did indeed carry the child of an elite vampire. The legacy member fell in love with the vampire that bit her, and he fell in love with her. After they broke the rule, it was discovered by what you might consider to be a counsel that upholds our laws."

"There's a vampire counsel?" I raised my eyebrows.

"The term is used rather loosely," he waved a dismissive hand. "The vampire was punished harshly and then sent to exile. The young woman, however, had already gone into hiding and was never located."

"Don't tell me… you're the vampire? And you're like my great-grandfather or something?"

"No," he chuckled. "If that were the case, I would not desire you as my bride, my dear."

"Well, at least there's some set of morals at play."

"We have our own code, or morals, you could say. They may not be what you'd expect, but we have them."

"Hmm. So, who was the vampire?" At least I could breathe easy knowing I wasn't somehow related to the vampire I had been hunting to kill. The vampire that had been hunting me to make me his bride. That would've been a bit too much for me to handle.

Count Vito gazed out a window for a moment before turning back to me. "He was a good friend named Lafayette. Much like an older brother to me. He made me promise that I would watch over his love and unborn child. Ensure the counsel never found her."

"I see. And then what happened?"

"The child grew up." He turned his gaze back to the window. "She knew she was from a legacy family, but never knew about her father. Unlike most children that survive, she had no fangs. She was apparently fully human, with her legacy blood blocking the vampire venom. She became a hunter. However, after her 18th birthday, she lost her temper in a fight against a vampire one evening. I was there, watching over her, and saw fangs emerge. They retracted when she regained her composure. It was the most curious thing. Something I'd never seen or heard of before. I'm not sure she even noticed, as she was so engrossed in her fight.

Eventually she married her hunting partner. They loved each other fiercely, and began a family. Unfortunately, they didn't live to see the family grow."

"Are you telling me that my… my mother was that child? The child of a legacy family and a vampire?"

He fixed his gaze on me for what felt like a solid minute before responding. "Yes, dear Kel. Your mother was the child I was meant to watch over. The child born of a legacy family and a vampire. And also where you get your temper from." A small chuckle.

I sat there, unable to respond. I was astonished, and the thoughts going through my head a mile a minute were completely jumbled and making no sense. One thought finally clicked.

"And that's why you brought me here on my 18th birthday? So you could watch for fangs like my mother?"

"Yes, that is one reason. However, I haven't seen you lose your temper enough for them to bare, despite my best attempts, unless you haven't inherited that trait. This is a rather different situation, so I can't say I know all of the details right now."

"And now," I began slowly, "you want me to be your bride?"

"That is correct."

"But you could have my blood and be set for the next hundred years, without me being your bride."

"Also correct."

"Then why?" It didn't make sense to me. Why would he pursue me as his bride when there was no necessity for it? A small, rueful smile appeared at his lips.

"It's time you learned the truth of what happened that night, dear Kel. The night you lost your parents. And what has occurred since then."

Chapter 18

I thought back to that fateful night – the night my parents were killed by a vampire. Killed by – Vito? No, that didn't seem right now, in light of what he told me. He was meant to protect my mother, so why would he kill her?

"Normally I did well, watching over your mother and ensuring her safety. No one knew she was from a legacy family except her. She never even told your father. One night, however, I had been out of town on business. Your parents had gone on a hunt that night, and a vengeful vampire followed them home. He had no desire for their blood, only their death.

"That night, the vampire did not bare his fangs. He went in with a pantera claw. Word was sent to me by my underlings who were tasked with watching her while I was away, and I returned as quickly as I could. However, the vampire was in a fit of rage, and had already clawed your parents to near death. They had lost too much blood to be saved. I arrived just as he turned towards you, an innocent child. He did not see an innocent child, though. Blinded by rage, he only wanted to kill."

"I remember… I remember being scared, thinking that was the end. I tried to run but tripped, and the next thing I knew, I was in your arms. You tucked me back in bed."

"That is correct."

"What happened to the vampire that killed my parents?" My gut twisted at this new knowledge. I had not spent my years hunting the vampire that had killed my parents. I had no idea who that vampire even was. I had wasted all this time.

"You must understand, my dear. Do not think poorly of me. I was enraged. I placed you back in bed and used my influence to have you enter a deep sleep. My servants had detained the vampire in the hall while I did so."

"What happened next?"

"I gave him a verbal lashing, explaining that it was a legacy family. His excuse was that he couldn't have known, because they were kept secret. That no one had ever said they were a protected family. That only enraged me further." He looked away at that point, back out the window. "I tore him limb from limb. I took a stake to his heart as he screamed in pain." That memory I had just had. It was that night. It was foggy because of the sleep he had induced.

"And you think I'd think poorly of you for that?"

He simply nodded. I sat in silence, as I took in all of this new information. The vampire I had been hunting should never have been my prey. The vampire that should have been my prey was in fact killed that very night by the vampire I thought I should be hunting. The vampire that had, in fact, been protecting me my entire life. The vampire that brought me together with Dustin. Dustin. How was this going to affect our relationship?

"I don't think poorly of you for it. I wish I had known earlier, so the vengeance and hatred wouldn't have had a chance to take hold of my heart."

"I should have told you. However, it was a very delicate situation. I thought it best to watch from afar and allow you to grow into whomever you were meant to grow into."

"But you never really watched from afar, did you? You were actually always close by."

"That is correct."

"But the way you've acted towards me during each of our meetings?" I left the question hanging, not really sure how to finish it.

"It was easier to have you close by, hunting me, than to have to chase you down regularly. If I openly showed favor, you would've eventually become suspicious."

I placed the book on the table and stood. "I should go."

"Dear Kel, do not be angry with me." Kel. Not hunter. The way in which he said my name was different from before. The truth was out, which also now changed our relationship in some way, I just wasn't sure how.

"I'm not. I just need to sort through all of this. Figure out how I feel about it."

"I will be here when you're ready to talk more about it."

He had said when. Not if. When I'm ready to talk. He was more confident that I'd want to talk about it than I was. Part of me wanted to bury this new information somewhere deep and not have to think about it. This was life changing information. I had no words, so I simply nodded my acknowledgment. He stood and led me to the massive front door.

"Goodbye, my Count." I had never called him "my" Count before. But it suddenly felt right. He had protected me my whole life. If nothing else, he was my protector.

"Farewell, my hunter. I will see you soon." A small smile played at his lips.

* * * * *

I slowly pushed open the front door to my home. The home I now shared with Dustin, my hunting partner. We became partners in part because we were both hunting for revenge on Vito. I couldn't even begin to imagine how all of this new information was going to change things between us. Or even how to begin telling him. I sighed and took a step inside. It was quiet.

"Dustin?"

"In here." I turned my head toward the living room, where I saw the tops of Dustin's feet resting on the arm of the sofa. I made my way over, still unsure of what to say to him. He turned off the TV and sat up as I sat in the armchair.

"I was starting to get worried. How'd it go? You find the book without that vamps coming for you?"

"Not exactly," I spoke hesitantly.

"You telling me he was there? Or you didn't find the book?"

I took a deep breath. I had to tell him everything now. Or at least, almost everything. *Maybe I'll still leave out the part about our conversations. I'm not sure he needs to know that.*

~I would agree.~

"Vito was there," I began. His eye twitched at my words. "And he had the book waiting for me."

"He knew you were going for it?"

"He knew. And he let me read the book."

"Without a fight?" He seemed incredulous.

"Without a fight. I learned a lot while there, if you'll let me talk." I smirked at him.

"Alright, alright," he raised his hands in surrender. "Sorry. I was just worried, and you come back and tell me that vamps was there waiting for you… I just thought the worst."

"I know. But it went nothing like what you'd expect. To start with, I've had it wrong all my life." Might as well start at the beginning.

"You had what wrong?"

"Vito didn't kill my parents." He opened his mouth to respond, but I held up my hand to quiet him. "It turns out, it was another vampire, and Vito was trying to protect my family. He saved my life-"

"Hold up. You're telling me that Vito was *protecting* your family? Why would a vampire do that?"

"Because you were partially right about legacy families."

"I was?" Dustin's eyes lit up with excitement. "Did his book talk about it? What did it say?" Although his research paper was about legacy families, no one had been able to confirm his information, so no information on legacy families was being taught in the Vampire Hunter Academy. This was cutting edge for humans.

"Legacy families do exist. And my mom was from a special one."

"Your mom? Then you're…?"

"Yes." I paused for a moment. "Did you know? Back when we spoke to Wally at The Raven, you said that he knew if he touched me, he'd die. Was it because of this?"

He stared at me, wide-eyed. "No. I sort of suspected at one point, because I knew that Count Vito had sent out some proclamation or whatever they called it. It was shortly after you graduated VHA, but he specifically said any female hunters were to be caught and brought to him unharmed. Wally would've known

150

that, for sure." He paused. "I had no way to confirm it, so I figured I was wrong and just forgot about it. But what do you mean your mom was from a special family? Aren't all legacy families special?"

"In a way, yes. And evidently vampires in the area of a legacy family know the family has a protected status, although I don't think they know why the family is protected and considered off limits. But my family was kept hidden, because of a huge secret. My mom's father wasn't exactly… normal," I finished rather lamely. Now that it was time to tell him, my words faltered. Trying to tell Dustin that my grandfather was a vampire was proving more difficult than I had imagined.

"What d'you mean by not normal? Wasn't he a legacy family, too?"

"No. He was a vampire."

"He was what?" Dustin practically jumped up from the sofa and stood there, staring at me as though he must've misheard me.

"My grandfather was a vampire. He fell in love with my grandmother, and against all odds they had a baby. My mother. But he paid a price for it and was exiled, and my grandmother had to go into hiding with my mother for safety."

"He was exiled and left them? So wait, Vito isn't your grandfather, is he?"

I let out a laugh. "No, he isn't. I wondered the same thing, actually. But it was a friend of Vito, and the friend asked Vito to watch over my grandmother and their baby. To protect them."

"Hang on." He slowly sat back down on the sofa. "Kel, how did you learn all this? Was all of this in the book?"

"No," I looked down to my lap. "The stuff about legacy families is in the book. But Vito had to fill in the blanks."

"And you believe the *vampire?*"

"I do. He told me what happened the night my parents died. He told me about the other vampire that killed my parents in a fit of rage. The vampire that turned to kill me, but Vito arrived in time to save me."

"Because you're legacy."

"And because of the promise to his friend."

Dustin sat back and took a few steadying breaths. I waited until he was ready for me to continue.

"After rescuing me, he killed the vampire that killed my parents. Then he continued to watch over me my whole life." I watched Dustin carefully as he began piecing everything together and saw the moment the realization hit him.

"He didn't kill your parents."

"No."

"He killed the vampire that killed your parents."

"Yes."

"You don't want to kill him anymore."

"No, I don't."

Silence. I didn't know what else I could say to him at this point, so I just waited and picked under my fingernails.

"I don't know how to feel about this, Kel. I still want to kill him."

"I know."

"He killed my brother."

"I know."

"But he saved you."

"Mm-hmm," I nodded, still looking down at my fingernails.

"Which means we never would've met if it weren't for… him."

The disdain in Dustin's voice didn't go unnoticed. I painfully realized that I had spoken of Vito my whole life with the same disdain in my voice. The man who had saved my life and protected me this whole time. *I'm so sorry.*

~It is fine, my dear. I wanted it that way so you wouldn't know.~

"But I still have to kill him."

"I know. But knowing what I know now… I can't help you with that anymore."

He abruptly stood up. "I'm going downstairs to train. It'll help me think. Maybe clear my head for a bit."

He turned and walked downstairs without another word. Not even another glance at me. I knew he was upset and hurt. But with how I was feeling, how could I continue to help him hunt the vampire that saved my life? Not only spared me like I had thought for years, but actually saved me? I turned the TV back on. Some reruns of an old show were playing. I stared at the TV, not seeing a thing. My thoughts were consumed with Vito, Dustin, and my parents.

152

My mother knew her legacy family heritage. Why hadn't she told me? Did she think I had been too young? She was probably right, but didn't I have a right to know this from her? Did she know about her father? I thought back to that fateful night, when my mother had told me to run. The small chamber in my closet was supposed to be a perfect hiding spot for me as a child. It was also where she had kept important papers and keepsakes. There was an old photo I remembered finding as a child. When I had showed it to my mother, she told me it was her as a child with her mother. She let me keep the photo. Because I had decided that it was important, I had hid it in the closet.

I stood up and went to my room. I wanted to look at my grandmother's photo again, knowing what I now knew. I opened the secret door in my closet and pulled out the pile of papers, rifling through until I found the photo. My grandmother's eyes looked straight at me. Nothing about her would've hinted that she had fallen in love with someone she shouldn't have. That she had rebelled. Nothing about my mother would've made one think that she had been the child of a vampire. I shuffled through the rest of the papers, looking for any other pictures. Instead, I found a letter addressed to me. I opened it up to read it.

Chapter 19

*D*ear Kel,

My sweet child. If you're reading this letter, then that means I am no longer with you. How are you my darling child? Are you growing up healthy? I love you so much. I am writing this letter in case something happens to me. I truly hope you never have to read this, but just in case, there is something I have to tell you. Our family is special. We are descendants of what is known as a "legacy family." That means we have special blood that protects us against vampires, however it also means that powerful vampires want our blood, because it enhances their abilities. But that's not all. My mother told me before passing away that there is something else that makes us truly special. You see, when she was younger, a vampire bit her. Her special blood kept her alive, but that wasn't the end for them. They fell in love. The result was a child – me. But many who knew were afraid it would turn out bad, just as other situations when a vampire and human have a child together. This was a first though – it's never happened with a legacy family. That's the only explanation my mother could come up with. So, I am the child of a legacy family and a vampire. Our family really is special.

I am so sorry I couldn't tell you this in person. My mother warned me of the dangers of anyone knowing, so I had decided I would tell you when you're old enough. There is one who can help, though. He is an elite vampire in the area named Count Vito. He was a friend of your grandfather, and my mother said if the need ever arose, we could go to him for help.

I love you so much, my sweet little girl. Please know that no matter what may have happened to me, I will always love you, and I am proud of you for going on and staying strong.

Love,
Mommy

P.S. If your father is still with you, he must never know about this. You must keep this secret, for his sake and especially for yours. I love him very much, but he may have a hard time understanding that vampire DNA runs through our blood as well.

I wiped away the tears that were streaming down my face. I had never actually looked through the papers my mother had in my closet hideaway before. Why would I? I was young when they were killed, and those papers were grown up things. I looked at the photo of my mother and grandmother again.

She knew. Her mother told her. This is irrefutable proof.

I heard the thud of footsteps coming up the stairs. Hastily, I shoved everything back into the compartment in my closet, keeping out only the letter, which I clutched close to my heart.

My mother told me. She trusted me enough to tell me. But she also said anyone knowing could be dangerous. And I've already told Dustin.

I heard the bathroom door shut, followed by the shower running. I carefully folded my letter back up and placed it in the bottom of the drawer of the nightstand next to my bed. My heart felt like leaping out of my chest. I had the words of my mother with me, always close to me. I hadn't known it, but a piece of her was always close by.

"I miss you, Mommy," I whispered. "I have grown up strong. I wish I had found this letter sooner, but I found out everything you wrote to me, thanks to Count Vito. He's been protecting me, so you don't need to worry. I love you."

I sat on my bed, grabbed my old teddy bear and allowed myself to cry some more. However, when I heard Dustin turn off the water, I forced myself to stop and be strong. The little girl in me missed her mother very much right now. But the grown hunter knew she had to keep moving forward. Dustin came out of the bathroom wearing a pair of cargo pants and a loose t-shirt, towel drying his hair. He peeked into my room.

"Hey." His voice had a bit of tension in it.

"Hey," I replied.

"Mind if I come in?"

"Of course not. Come on in."

He came in and sat on the edge of my bed, seemingly keeping his distance. *Did I mess up by telling him? No,* I thought, *I can trust him.*

"Listen," he began. "I can't imagine how you're feeling right now. I'm reeling from everything you told me, and it's not like it's all about me and my family or anything. I know you probably have a lot to think about. But," he hesitated.

"But what?"

"While you were gone, I got a call. There's a hunting party tonight. They're going after Vito, and I already said I'd join them. I won't back out now. I still want my revenge on him. But I won't ask you to join us."

"Thanks. I really don't think I'd be able to at this point. Not now that I know…" That explained the cargo pants. He was wearing typical clothes for a night of hunting.

"I know. And it's fine. But I have to go with them. Not only do we know his location, but they said they have someone to help the hunting party that should guarantee our win. I have to get going. Gotta meet the gang at The Raven to prep before we head out."

"I'm just gonna chill here tonight. Maybe take a night off, play some video games or something."

"Ok," he stood. "You relax tonight. And Kel?"

"Yeah?"

"I love you."

"I love you, too." My voice was somewhat constricted. I knew I could trust him. He hadn't stopped loving me just because we learned my DNA was different.

"Be back later."

"See you then."

He turned and walked downstairs, then after a few minutes I heard the front door close.

What do I do? I dropped my head into my hands. *I feel so torn right now. As a vampire hunter, I should be glad for this. But do I even want to be a hunter anymore? My reason for hunting was to kill the vampire that killed my parents. He's already been killed. What reason do I have for hunting now?*

~Calm yourself, my dear. I can hear your thoughts from here.~ Vito.

~You sound a bit surprised.~

I just wasn't expecting you. I need to talk to you. In person. Please.

Just like that, he appeared in my room at my request. I could never get past the weirdness of a vampire needing to be invited into a home in order to enter like this. Such a powerful creature, needing permission. How had he entered all this time, though? All those times I hadn't invited him in? Had my mother given him permission before her death? He sat on the edge of my bed, where Dustin had been just minutes before. The thought gave me a hollow feeling in my stomach.

"Here I am, my dear. What is so urgent?"

"They're coming for you. Tonight. Dustin went to join a hunting party. He said they have someone who will guarantee their win against you."

"I see. And you are not joining them this time?"

"You know I can't," I looked away from him, towards the window.

"You've made your choice, then."

"What choice?" I looked back at him. Did he know the battle I was having with myself right now?

"I told you yesterday you have choices to make, although it may not be the choices you thought you'd be having to make. It would appear that you have chosen to no longer be a hunter."

Yup. He knew the battle I was having. Of course he did. He probably knew I'd have this battle long before I could ever even imagine questioning my desire to be a hunter.

"I haven't decided for sure. I just know I can't hunt *you* now. Not now that I know everything." I looked down at my teddy bear. The one connection I had felt to my parents for so long. The connection that had kept me grounded my whole life. Vito moved closer and lifted my chin with his hand.

"I suppose I can no longer call you 'dear hunter,'" he chuckled. "I appreciate your concern. I promise you I will not let anything happen to me. I must protect you."

"Yeah, I know. The promise you made to your friend."

"I'm afraid I did not tell you everything earlier. I'm not entirely sure you're ready to hear it." He dropped his hand from my chin and sat up straight once more.

"Tell me. I don't want anything else kept from me."

"The promise to my friend is only part of my reason for protecting you. Indeed, if that were my only reason, I likely would not have gone to the lengths I have in order to protect you so entirely."

"What do you mean?"

"I watched you grow up. I have felt an immense connection with you since your parents were killed. I always knew the connection was related to my feelings of failure in my promise to my friend. However, as you continued to grow, I realized I was enjoying watching you become a young woman. It was more than my promise. Like my friend, I had a vulnerability."

"What vulnerability?"

"You, dear Kel. I do not want you as my bride because of your legacy family status. I desire you as my bride because I love you."

And once again, I found myself sitting in silence. Not waiting for someone else to get over a shocking detail this time, but because I was the one who was shocked. My brain seemed unable to process his words, despite having heard them clearly.

"I have had plenty of time to come to terms with my feelings for you, and I would hardly ask you to decide how you feel tonight, after having so much weight placed upon you. However," he stood as he spoke now, "I will protect you because of how I feel about you. And to do so, I must not let anything happen to me."

"I – I mean, I…"

"No, my dear. Do not try to make sense of it now. Sleep, and allow yourself to look at it in the morning with fresh eyes. I will be waiting when you are ready to speak once again. For now, I think it best that your mind be at ease. I hear you most easily when you are feeling distressed."

He smiled gently at me as I felt my eyes grow heavy. Did he use his powers on me, like he had when he saved me as a child? What was going to happen tonight? Dustin was going to hunt Vito, and Vito had said some time ago that he would have me as his bride. But Dustin and I were together now. Would Vito kill Dustin tonight? No, I couldn't let that happen. I couldn't…

* * * * *

I bolted up in my bed. Everything around me was dark. Either Vito's powers were growing weaker, or I had gained some resiliency to them. Glancing at the clock showed me it was a little after two in the morning. I heard some light commotion going on downstairs. *Dustin? It has to be. He has to be ok.*

Gingerly, I stepped out of bed. I still felt a little groggy. After effects of Vito's power, no doubt. I walked slowly downstairs, and heard hushed voices in the living room. Some voices I didn't recognize, so I decided it would be better to assess the situation than to give myself away and ask for possible trouble.

"This was your doing. He knew we were coming. He was ready for us."

"I didn't say a word. Trust me, the only way I can escape him at this point is for him to die. I want him dead just as much as Dustin does." A female voice I recognized. I held my breath, waiting for more information, despite wanting to go in there and confront her. I had to know that Dustin was ok first.

"It wouldn't be the first time you betrayed us, Claudia. You can't blame him for suspecting you."

"I know. And you know I always look out for myself. What benefit would I gain from Vito knowing we were on our way to kill him?"

"None," groaned Dustin.

"Hey, lay down, man." I recognized Brian's voice from The Raven. "You took a beating for me. No more playing tough guy."

"Who's playing?" A small chuckle accompanied Dustin's strained voice. I decided that it was time for me to make an appearance.

"Hey, if it isn't Kel. Sorry you couldn't join us tonight. Feeling better now?" Brian had a smile on his face as I made my way into the living room.

"Much, thanks." I guess Dustin told them I was sick to explain my absence. At least for now my secret was still safe. I walked around to the front of the couch. "What happened? And give me one good reason why *she* is in my house." I jabbed my thumb in the direction of Claudia.

Dustin looked up at me, his face bloody and bruising. "Yeah, remember when I said we had someone who thought they could guarantee our win?"

"It was *her*?" I narrowed my eyes at him. I remembered our last encounter, and as far as I was concerned, I still couldn't trust her.

"Yeah," he coughed. "Sorry. I knew you wouldn't like hearing that, so I just kinda left that part out."

"I'm standing right here, you know." Claudia had placed her hands on her hips, obviously annoyed that we were speaking about her as if she couldn't hear us.

"Yeah, I know," I snapped my head over to look at her. "The last time we met, you told me we would be enemies when we saw each other next. So why exactly would I trust you now?"

"Because you gave me a lot to think about last time."

My eyes softened. "And?"

"And I don't want to play for the other team. But the only way I can get out of my deal is if the other party is dead. Not undead, but completely dead."

"I see." The last time we saw each other, I probably would've jumped in to help her with this plan. But now? There had to be another way. I felt now like I owed my life to Vito, several times over. "And Dustin? What happened to you? I thought you were going to start being more careful! Now look at you. A bloody mess. Again." I turned on my heel to grab a bowl of water and washcloth from the kitchen. I heard him chuckle as I walked away.

"Don't mind her. I've been kinda sloppy lately, so she's probably getting tired of cleaning me up." I could practically see the grin on his face.

"You got that right," as I sat in front of the sofa with the bowl of water. I started wiping away gently at the blood. "Did Vito do this to you?"

"One of his underlings," Brian said. "The guy was coming after me, actually, but Dustin jumped in the way 'cause my back was turned. Probably saved my life, if I have to be honest."

At least Vito didn't target Dustin.

~I wouldn't. I know the pain that would cause you.~

And you! Are you ok?

~Is that concern I hear in your thoughts, my dear?~

Just answer the question. I'm mad at you right now.

~Fair enough. Yes, I am well.~

Good. Now goodnight. I was sure my annoyance was portrayed well in my thoughts. I was angry he forced me to sleep. I was unable to do anything to help either of the men I cared deeply about. I may not want to be a hunter anymore, but that didn't mean I couldn't protect what I held dear.

"Alright then, that's that. So what now?" One of the other guys I recognized from The Raven spoke up. I didn't really know anything about him, but recognized his voice as the one who accused Claudia of warning Vito.

"Now what?" Claudia laughed. It was a short, derisive laugh. "Now I die. Simple as that. The Count saw me with you all tonight. It goes against the deal we made, and the rules were clear: if I broke the deal, it would result in my death. This was my last chance at life."

Is that true? Claudia is going to die because she broke her deal with you?

~It is code.~

It's wrong.

"There must be another way," I said softly.

"At this point, Kel, it's kill or be killed."

You're going to kill her? I gently pulled at my lower lip, contemplative.

~No. The binding magic of the contract will.~

Isn't there anything…?

~There is, however you won't like it.~

I didn't like his response. I had no idea what their contract entailed, but I had a feeling that he was right – whatever she could do to avoid the broken contract, I probably wasn't going to like it.

"Claudia, what do you have to do in order to fulfill your part of the bargain?"

She turned toward me then, to face me full on. "Do you remember our last encounter? At the castle?"

"The castle?" Dustin asked. "What are you talking about?"

"You didn't tell Dustin?"

"Of course not," I looked down at Dustin. "You would've stood in my way, and I had to get some information."

"When was this? What-" Dustin was obviously taken aback, but Claudia shushed him.

"That's not important now. What is important, Kel, is that I wasn't entirely truthful."

"About?"

"I told you that Vito wanted nothing to do with you, but was actually after Dustin. I lied."

"I figured."

"In order to fulfill my contract, I must deliver you to him."

"So take me to him."

"You don't understand," she looked me dead in the eye. "I must deliver you to him as his bride."

Chapter 20

Dustin sat up on the sofa with help from Brian. The effort it took was obviously tremendous. He stared directly at Claudia as I looked over at him. Beaten, bloody, bruised, and determined. His face told me he'd rather let Claudia meet her death than hand me over as a vampire bride.

"Not happening," Dustin said through gritted teeth.

"I know," Claudia hung her head as she spoke. "I wouldn't ask that of her now anyway."

"Why? You always look out for yourself," the guy I didn't know sneered. He was full of disdain for Claudia. She raised her eyes to meet his.

"Because Kel was the first person to treat me like a human being in a long time. To act as though I could be worth something."

"Lighten up, Johnny," Dustin said. I looked over to him to see his eyes had softened a bit.

"Yeah, well," Johnny mumbled and looked away.

"How much time do we have left before you're in breach of your contract?" Brian spoke up, acting as the voice of reason.

"Typically a person has twenty-four hours from the initial breach of contract to set things right, or the magic will take them. My initial breach took place yesterday, when I came to you with my plan. So that leaves me with," she paused as she checked the clock and ran through her time frame. "About eight hours." Her voice faltered as the finality of it hit her. I looked at the clock. Almost three in the morning.

"So that's about eight hours to plan an attack and execute it. Not only execute it, but execute it in a way that ensures success."

"It's a suicide mission," Johnny grumbled.

"Count me in," grinned Dustin.

"No you don't, man." Brian. The voice of reason.

"I can manage."

"No," Brian gently pushed back on Dustin, who fell back on the sofa with a grunt, "you can't."

With a concerted effort, Dustin sat back up, then slowly stood. "Yes. I can. I have to. This vampire has already taken enough from me. I'm not gonna sit here and wait while he takes away the only other people I freaking care about!"

"Don't argue with him Brian," I said. "You know better. When Dustin decides he's going to do something, he throws caution to the wind and does whatever he wants."

Brian side eyed Dustin for a moment before nodding once. He then pushed Dustin back down to the sofa. "Fine, but you're resting while we plan. Otherwise I'll tie your sorry butt to this sofa while we have all the fun," he smirked.

"Deal," Dustin groaned.

"Let the planning begin," Johnny said. He actually looked excited instead of angry now.

"Thank you, everyone," Claudia's barely audible voice came from her drooped head and sagging shoulders.

"Not doing this for you, chick," Johnny said. "I just wanna kill the vampire."

"Honestly," Brian said, "I'm doing this for Dustin."

"I know. But still, thank you."

"Well," I said with a heavy sigh. "You start planning. I'll go make some pizza rolls. Can't plan on an empty stomach, right?"

A general agreeance sounded from the group. I made my way over to the kitchen, knowing I wouldn't be any help in planning this time anyway. I wasn't going to help them come up with a way to kill Vito. I knew one thing for sure though: whatever plan they came up with, they'd have to have a contingency plan. Even if I didn't tell Vito a thing, he'd probably know what to expect.

The thought of Vito had me torn as I spread the pizza rolls on a baking sheet. Here these hunters were, plotting away to finally kill him. He's a vampire, so he needed to be killed anyway. Humans would never truly be safe unless we could rid the world of vampires entirely. But I also owed him my life. I wouldn't be able to kill him now. And how could I worm my way out of the hunting party, now that they knew I wasn't sick?

~It is a dilemma, isn't it my dear?~

Are you going to be helpful?

~I would love nothing more. However, this one is entirely on you. I will enjoy seeing you again, though. I do believe this will be the most times we've seen each other in such a short time frame.~

Are you messing with me right now?

~Perhaps a little.~ I could hear his chuckle in my mind.

Shouldn't you be busy preparing as well?

~I have already prepared.~

"Got anything to drink?" Brian came up behind me, tearing me from my hushed conversation.

"Yeah, we got some soda and water in the fridge. I can make some coffee if you need it."

"Coffee sounds good. Gonna need all we can get to pull this off." He sighed. "I'm worried about Dustin," he spoke softly, so Dustin wouldn't hear him.

"Me, too. He's not really in any condition to be going back in so soon."

"Not only that, but I've seen this look in his eyes before. Right after his brother was killed."

"What happened?"

"He went ballistic. And I don't have to tell you how dangerous that is when fighting the undead."

I nodded. Keeping your wits about you in a fight against the undead was one of the biggest components. You lose that and you're likely to lose your life. These weren't mindless creatures we were up against. I started going about making the coffee.

"So how do we keep him safe? Keep him alive?"

"I'm not sure. We're talking about gathering some more hunters. Hoping sheer numbers will do the trick. But we gotta find a way to keep Dustin to the back. I know he's got a vendetta against this Count, and he's a good hunter. But he lets his emotions set him off like a loose cannon sometimes. We can't afford that if we're going to win this one."

"Hmm." We stood in silence as the coffee maker began dripping hot coffee into the carafe. "What if I twist my ankle? Like early into the fight. He'd stay behind to protect me, I think." I wasn't entirely sure at this point, but I thought it might help me kill two birds with one stone. I could keep Dustin alive by keeping him back, and I could bow out of the fight.

"Maybe," Brian replied doubtfully. "A twisted ankle isn't much, though. He may just sit you somewhere and tell you to be careful."

"True." I grabbed a couple of plates and then took the pizza rolls out of the oven, splitting them between the two plates. "Maybe..."

"Maybe what?"

"Maybe Claudia can help."

"I doubt it. She only looks out for herself. Heck, only reason I think any of us are even willing to help her is really because she's been able to give us information to use against Count Vito. None of us really like her. Especially Dustin."

"Yeah, I know their history." *I also know something you don't know. She still loves him. And Dustin... he may not love her anymore, but part of him still cares about her. I know I saw it in his eyes.*

"Then you know this is a painful gathering right now. The sooner we move it along, the sooner Dustin can rest and relax a bit."

"Take these plates out there and send Claudia in. Tell her I need help prepping the coffee or something."

Brian looked at me and raised an eyebrow. He knew I was planning something, but he seemed to think better of prying me for information. He took the plates out and told Claudia to help me with the coffee. She appeared at my side after a quick moment. One look at my face and she knew something was up.

"What is it?"

"I need your help keeping Dustin away from the fight." I began taking coffee cups out of the cupboard and lining them up on the counter to distract myself.

"You want me to keep Dustin away from your precious Count, is that it?" she laughed.

"No, I want you to help me keep Dustin alive. I know that's what you want, because I know you still care deeply about him. And that's why you're going to help me. Now stop this defensive act and listen."

My assertiveness must've taken her by surprise, because her face softened and she nodded.

"Thank you. Now, I think Dustin will hang back if I'm injured. I don't want to get seriously hurt for real, in case I need to defend myself. But can you use your magic to make it appear like I got hurt?"

"I could. I could create a sort of vampire mirage to attack you."

"Good. It would need to attack me hard enough that Dustin stays back with me. He needs to feel like he has to watch over me and defend me."

"He won't like it if he figures out what we're doing, you know." She began pouring coffee into the cups I had set on the counter.

"I know. So he can't find out."

Claudia stared at me for a moment, contemplating something. Finally, she seemed satisfied with her thoughts and nodded her agreement before grabbing a couple of mugs to take out to the group. They continued talking as I set about cooking another batch of pizza rolls. I knew what I had to do to keep Dustin safe. But I was still torn about Vito. Years of hunting screamed at me about our need to be rid of vampires. *But I have vampire blood, too. Does that mean the world needs to be rid of me as well?*

I took a couple more cups of coffee out to the living room.

"Yeah, uh-huh. Anyone available would help. Thanks, man." Brian hung up his phone. "Most of the hunters are out on other hunts right now. Hank said he's got three or four guys to spare, but that's it."

"You sure about this entry point, Claudia?" Johnny still seemed skeptical.

"Yes."

"I trust her, Johnny," Dustin said, popping a pizza roll into his mouth. "The question now is, once we get there and the party gets started, who gets to go in this entry point and after Vito?"

"I know you want to, Dustin. But you're pretty banged up. Maybe let me take this one?" Brian suggested.

"I wouldn't trust anyone to do it more than you, man." They clanked their coffee mugs together and took a sip.

"So it's a surprise attack, then?" I inquired.

"Yeah, Claudia's been in the castle a little while and knows of a back entry point. That vampire won't be expecting this."

"We're going to get him this time, Kel. Then maybe take a vacation and relax for a change," Dustin smiled. I half-smiled back and nodded before going back to the kitchen for the next batch of pizza rolls. I had a gnawing feeling in my stomach. I knew what I needed to do. I had the plan in place. Now I just needed to follow through for my final hunt.

My final hunt.

~Is that sorrow I hear in your thoughts, my dear?~

Maybe a little. This will be the last time we meet like this, you know. After this, I'm officially quitting as a vampire hunter.

~Even if things don't go according to their plan?~

No matter what.

~Interesting.~

I took the pizza rolls out of the oven and put them on plates to take out once again. Every single thing I was doing felt surreal. Less than a day from now, I would no longer be Kel the vampire hunter. I would just be plain old Kel.

~There is nothing plain about you, dear Kel.~ I walked into the living room with the plates of food.

To you, maybe. To the world? I'll probably be another burnt out hunter. No big.

Claudia watched as I entered the room. She seemed to be suspicious of something, so I just grabbed the empty plates and went back to the kitchen. Unfortunately, she followed me.

"What's going on, Kel?"

"What do you mean?"

"Why aren't you out there planning with them?"

"They need food and caffeine to keep going right now. They'll catch me up on their plans before we go. And you and I already have our own plan, anyway."

"Yeah, but…" she narrowed her eyes at me.

"But what?" I put the plates on the counter and looked at her, challenging her with my eyes.

"You had a look in your eyes just now. A look I recognize."

"Oh?"

"One that humans often get when someone is speaking in their mind. It's a subtle look, but to the trained eye, we can recognize it."

"I dunno what you're talking about. I'm tired, and getting over being sick. Maybe that's the look you're seeing?"

"You don't have to admit it to me, Kel," she placed her hand on my shoulder. "But, if you're talking to Vito, please make sure you aren't putting all of us in danger by doing so."

"I'm not," I said. "Talking to Vito, I mean. Why would I?"

She sighed. "Ok, if you say so. I'll go grab the coffee cups for refills."

I watched her walk back to the living room and let out my breath. *How did she know? And she looked scared that I may be talking to him and putting her life in danger. It's like... she's scared to die.*

Claudia walked back into the kitchen with the empty coffee mugs, and a slightly incredulous look on her face. "I think we may need to make more coffee. They've all finished and four more hunters are on their way. Do they always drink this much coffee?"

I sighed and lifted my eyes towards the ceiling. "Yeah. Y'know, this is not what I expected when Dustin and I decided to use my house as home base. Cooking and making coffee for everyone. If you can call making pizza rolls cooking." I let out a short laugh.

"Yeah," she laughed. "Not exactly action packed right now, huh?"

"Nope," I laughed. "Oh well. I guess it's the calm before the storm."

"A big storm, at that."

"Kel, Claudia, come on in here," Dustin called. I left the coffee to brew. We went into the living room, where Brian proceeded to detail our plans for the fight. I noticed the four other hunters had arrived already. No doubt looking forward to the biggest fight of their careers. This is what it meant to be a vampire hunter.

"And then, once you all have his cronies fully engaged in battle, Claudia will get me in through the back. We should be able to sneak up on him from behind while he's busy calling out orders. He's also likely going to be watching for Kel, and his chance to snatch her, which should give us the upper hand. Alright, that's about the jist of it. Let's check over our weapons and head out. Let's say about one hour?"

A general murmur of agreeance, as the tension levels rose. I could feel the excitement and nervousness filling the room. This was it. The beginning of the biggest battle of our lives. And maybe even the ends of some of our lives.

Chapter 21

"Alright, the castle is around the bend in the road there, then up the mountain just a ways. Everyone know their role?" Brian took up the role of command as soon as the other hunters had arrived, and it seemed to suit him. The whole group listened without batting an eye.

"Dustin, we know the Count wants Kel, so I want you to make sure you bring up the rear with her. We ain't giving him what he wants, got it?"

"Yeah, man, I got it." Dustin understood, but he didn't like being out of the major action. Still, he stood close enough to me that I could feel his fingers twitch towards his weapon. I knew he understood the importance of his assignment, but I also knew him well enough to know that as soon as the fight broke out, he'd rush right in. I glanced over to Claudia and caught her eye, nodding once. She returned my nod. Our deal was still on. Good.

The pack of hunters began moving forward, weapons of all sorts drawn and at the ready. Swords, daggers, guns, and even a whip with blessed silver braided into it. As we entered the gate, Brian and Claudia split off to make their way to the back entrance for their sneak attack. Moments after they split off, a few dozen vampires began their attack. We fought them off well, but were definitely outnumbered. Dustin quickly started advancing, a hunger in his eyes and adrenaline masking his pain. Claudia was almost out of sight now. She glanced back once and saw me watching her. With a flick of her wrist, a mirage of a vampire appeared mere feet from me. I made a show of fighting it, and called out for Dustin just before I was thrown backwards into a tree.

I felt the wind knock out of me. Whether she meant it to hurt or not, being thrown by magic was always painful. Being thrown into a tree doubly so. Dustin came running back to my side, as the vampire mirage ran off into the trees and literally disappeared.

"Kel! Kel, are you ok?" He helped me sit up as I worked to take a couple of deep breaths.

"Yeah, I just need a second to catch my breath. That freaking hurt."

"I'm sorry, it's my fault. I was supposed to be next to you."

"It's fine, you're here now. Help me stand up."

He offered me his hand and with a grunt helped me stand. He turned to face the castle again, this time advancing slower and making sure I was close by. We continued to fight off vampires from the sides as the group progressed closer to the castle. As we finally approached the steps, Vito made his appearance on the balcony above.

"Pitiful hunters, did you think I wouldn't expect you? You have no chance of victory here." He looked around to his vampire soldiers and addressed them. "Remember your orders well, or the price will be high!" He disappeared back into the castle as more vampires converged on our group. Dustin and I fell back into a defensive position to cover the rear, which proved mostly useless. Hardly any vampires came towards us for a direct attack.

"Kel, this is his plot. He's trying to get to you. He wants you unharmed, so I'll bet-" He swung his katana at a vampire closing in on us. "I'll bet he's ordered them not to hurt you, just capture. Stay close to me." I nodded and pulled out my dagger. I liked getting close to the vampires as I killed them, so I chose my favorite dagger for tonight. At least I could make my final hunt a fruitful one. We slowly inched our way up the front steps and into the castle, where vampires with more fighting experience were waiting for us.

"No!" I heard Claudia scream. I looked up to see Vito on the second floor landing, Claudia and Brian captured and held by vampire soldiers in front of him.

"Did you truly think I wouldn't know of your subterfuge? That I wouldn't know you planned to sneak in and try to attack from behind? Cowardly woman."

Claudia glared at him, but a tear fell down her cheek. "Just kill me now. Show mercy and kill me quickly, before the magic does."

"And why would I do that?"

"Because I at least brought her here."

Vito looked down at me for a moment. "That's not enough to redeem you, witch, and you know it."

"Which is why I am asking only that you kill me quickly. Give me this one kindness."

"Take her down to the dungeon," Vito instructed the vampire who held Claudia. I understood his intentions – he would do as she asked. He would kill her quickly, but his glance down at me told me that he didn't want to do so in front of me.

Something in my mind clicked. I had never actually seen him kill, despite knowing that he had killed before. He had never let me see it. He thought I would think poorly of him because of how he killed the vampire that murdered my parents. I felt my blood run hot. Claudia didn't deserve to die, and I had to save her. Vito's words echoed in my mind: *"I desire you as my bride because I love you."* My brain finally processed those words.

You love me.

Vito turned his attention fully to me then, as the fight continued around me.

You've protected me my whole life because you love me, not just because of the promise. You don't want me as a bride because of my blood. It's because you love me. You were telling the truth.

~You've finally figured it out, dear hunter. Unfortunately, it is still too late for Claudia. I cannot save her now. The magic is final.~

But you'll honor her wish and kill her quickly?

~And as painlessly as possible, if that is your wish.~

I stared into his eyes from below for a moment. I didn't want Claudia to suffer. As much as we may have had tensions between us, I didn't believe her to be entirely evil. Just a little too worried about her own sense of safety. My blood continued to pulse hard through my veins, allowing me to feel the rush.

Allow me to approach.

"I call for a short parley. If you hunters will cease momentarily, I shall have my soldiers pause as well."

"We accept," I replied quickly, before any hunters could tell him off.

"Kel, what are you doing?" Dustin turned to me, surprised.

"Dustin, I love you. But this isn't going to work, and we both know it."

"We're doing fine, what are you talking about? He's taking huge casualties."

"Not that. You know my status," I whispered in his ear. "I planned to quit being a hunter. But you? You've got a lot of fight left."

"What are you planning?" I saw the apprehension in his eyes as he spoke.

"I'm saving everyone here tonight. Myself included."

"I grow tired of waiting, hunter. Are we to speak or shall we continue the fight?" Vito spoke in a commanding voice that I now realized was just a show for his underlings and the hunters.

"We're to speak." I kissed Dustin on the cheek. "Get Claudia out of here, and take care of her. She's a pain, but she loves you, too. And she's not as strong as she pretends to be."

I walked away before Dustin could stop me and slowly made my way up the stairs. I saw Johnny inch his way closer to Dustin and start whispering to him. No doubt asking if I had gone insane or something. Maybe I had. I was approaching the most powerful vampire in our area, and I wasn't even feeling an ounce of fear. Yes, I probably had gone insane.

"Are you wanting to come to an agreement to cease this battle, hunter?"

"I am."

"And what do you have to offer that would convince me to do so?"

"Me."

All eyes were on me now, and I could feel their shock. But the only eyes I was looking into were Vito's. Even his eyes showed surprise at my words.

"You would offer yourself to save these hunters?"

"And Claudia. Her deal with you was to bring me to you as your bride, correct?"

"That is correct."

"She brought me here. And I am ready to be your bride. So that should fulfill her end of the contract as well."

"Is this truly your choice? You wish to sacrifice yourself for her?"

"Yes," I replied. *I don't see it as a sacrifice, though.*

"Kel, no!" Brian yelled. "That wasn't part of the plan, what are you thinking?"

~I see. You wish to put on a show for your fellow hunters. To live on through this sacrifice?~ He made a show of staring me down, as if considering the possibility of this being a ploy to get in close for the kill shot.

Not quite. I want to put on a show and keep them from ever learning the truth about my blood.

"Brian, look around. This is what will result in the least amount of hunter blood spilled. We don't have a chance at winning. They still outnumber us."

"But-"

"Forget it, Brian," Dustin called angrily up to him. "She's as bad as me. When she makes up her mind, there is no listening to reason or logic."

I knew Dustin was hurt, and it made me want to cry. I did love him so much, but I also realized that he would never be able to truly accept the fact that I had vampire blood running through my veins as well.

"Very well, hunter. I accept your offer. For my part, I order my servants to release the hunters, as well as Claudia."

Can I say goodbye to Dustin?

~Very well.~

I walked back down the stairs, holding my head as high as I could, despite the pain in my heart. I watched Dustin as he kept his eyes on me the whole time, his chest heaving with each breath. Quickening my pace, I practically ran to him and embraced him tight.

"I am so sorry, Dustin. Can you ever forgive me?"

"What's to forgive?" he asked and hugged me tight. "The fact that you're leaving me for a vampire? Or that you think I should go back to a crazy ex-girlfriend?" I felt a sob escape from him.

"I love you, Dustin. But I really think this is best for everyone now. It's the only way to save Claudia's life. Maybe it'll even give her a reason to change her behaviors."

He laughed at that. "Kel, why can't you ever stop and just do what makes you and I happy? Stop worrying about others all the time?"

I pulled back and looked at him with a small smile on my face. "Because I've known my whole life I would either kill Vito or be killed by him. I can't kill him now. And he won't kill me. The next option is this. It'll also allow me to keep my family's secret."

"Would you stop making it so hard to be mad at you?" Dustin cried. Tears began streaming down his face. It was only then that I realized I had been crying, too.

"I love you, Dustin. Get the team out of here. And Claudia. She puts on a show, but it's because she doesn't like looking weak."

"I'll get her out of here, but then that's it."

I made a small sound to indicate that I understood what he meant. He'd honor my wish and get her to safety, but there was no way he was going to take care of her after that. As he had said, she was a crazy ex-girlfriend. And now vampire was added to the mix.

"Come, hunter, before I decide to call the deal off." *~Her time is almost up.~*

I nodded. Grabbing Dustin's hand, I gave it a tight squeeze before kissing him gently on the lips and then made my way back up the stairs.

"In order to save the life of Claudia, the deal must be sealed before the contract claims her."

"You mean the marriage has to happen… now?"

"Kel, don't do it!" Claudia called from downstairs as soon as she had been brought up from the basement. "It's ok. I'm ready to die."

"No, Claudia. This is my choice." I turned back to Vito. "So, this happens now? Like, right now?"

"Indeed. We will swear ourselves to each other in front of our fellow vampires and hunters alike. That will complete the contract with Claudia, and she shall be free."

"Gee, and to think I left all my good dresses hanging up at home." My nerves were getting to me. I hadn't expected things to happen this quickly. I had barely made the decision and already I was going to be married. Vito chuckled.

"Worry not, my dear," he whispered into my ear. "We can have a proper ceremony later, if you'd like."

"Mm. I'm just nervous. I didn't expect it to happen so fast. I thought I'd have a little more time to process this."

"Perhaps a change of clothes would calm your nerves. Maybe something not covered in blood?"

I looked down at my shirt and pants, which were indeed covered in blood. Not waiting for an answer, he led me to the rooms he had called my chambers for so long now. "Any dress of your choosing, dearest. I shall wait out here."

He closed the bedroom door behind him, leaving me alone in the large room. I couldn't believe I had actually agreed to this. What *was* I thinking? I made my way into the closet and glanced at the dresses. I saw the red velvet dress I had worn the first time I was here, and decided that was the perfect dress for this. I peeled off my bloody clothes in the attached bathroom and wiped myself down before sliding the dress over my head. Sparkly heels finished the look, and I let my hair out of my usual, now messy, ponytail before exiting the bedroom.

Vito stood right outside the door, and offered his hand the moment I emerged. A smile and nod told me he approved of my choice in dress. We stepped up to the edge of the balcony and he took both of my hands in his, facing me toward him.

"Kel, is it your promise to wed me and spend eternity with me?"

I took a deep breath. This was it. The moment I had feared for so long. It was a different sort of scary now, but still my insides twisted. "It is," I said, making sure I was loud enough that all present could hear.

"It is also my promise to wed you and spend eternity with you. With this, we are now wed." He slipped an old fashioned diamond ring onto my finger. I couldn't help but wonder where he had gotten it from. And how long did he have it on him? Did he grab it while I had been changing?

"Claudia?" Dustin's voice rang from downstairs. "What's wrong? Are you ok?"

"Yeah," she said as she leaned on him. "Just drained. The magic of the contract has left my body. It just takes a lot out of you."

"And with this, the contract is fulfilled. All hunters are officially no longer welcome. You may leave now, or face the consequences. My servants: we shall honor our end of the deal. No harm shall come to them as they leave."

Not a single mouth made a sound as the hunters gathered together at the door. I only just noticed that Brian was downstairs with them. He narrowed his eyes as he looked up at me once more before walking outside. But I only spared him a glance before my eyes settled on Dustin, helping to support Claudia as she walked out with the team. He was my hunting partner for so long now, and the first real relationship I had ever had. I knew right then that he would always hold a special place in my heart.

Epilogue

As the great door thudded to a close, Count Vito turned to me.

"You are mine now, my dear, and I am thrilled at that. But are you happy with your choice?"

"I am, I think. For so long, I've felt out of place. I realize now that here, I feel like in a weird sort of way, I belong. I felt it when you let me read that book, I just didn't understand it yet."

"And your hunting partner?"

"He'll be ok," my voice quivered. "He's strong, and has a good team around him. They'll take care of him."

"And I will take care of you, Countess," Vito raised my hand to his lips and placed a gentle kiss there, causing me to catch my breath.

"Do not worry," he laughed. "I will not change you until you are ready, should that day ever come. However, as my bride, you now hold the title of Countess either way." He led me to my rooms and held the door open for me. I walked in, more than a little nervous.

"And now, my dear, it is time for something truly important."

"And that is?" I felt my heart pounding in my chest. I hadn't really thought things through when I had decided to become his bride and what all that would entail.

"You rest. I know you've been awake all night, and it's most likely been a tiring day thus far." He laughed as he noticed the look on my face. "You needn't worry. All in due time, at your own pace. I've waited countless years for you already. A little longer won't kill me."

I entered my closet and picked out a pair of comfortable pants and a shirt before reentering my bed chamber. Vito gestured me toward my private bathroom, which I gratefully entered so I could take a quick shower. As I climbed into the bed, my hair still damp, I gazed around, reminding myself that this was my home now. Vito turned to leave.

"Vito?"

"Yes, my dear?" He turned his head toward me.

"Will you stay here?"

"Of course," he said, his eyebrows raised. It must've come as a shock, after so many years of misplaced anger. He sat on the edge of my bed as I settled in and reached for his hand. I understood now that I really hadn't been alone my whole childhood, and the presence that I always felt and had never understood was the presence of this man here, keeping me safe from any harm. I felt a sense of security wash over me as my eyes drifted shut.

When I opened my eyes again, I was greeted by a smile from Vito's face. I sat up and rubbed the sleep from my eyes. Had he stayed by my side the whole time I slept?

"Are you well rested?"

"Yeah, I think so."

"Then rise, Countess. We have a celebration tonight."

"What celebration?"

"Tonight I shall present you to my kind as my bride. We begin your life as Countess this very evening, where those who serve me shall also pledge fealty to you. Tomorrow begins a new chapter in your life, where you will start learning more about the vampire world than you ever imagined. You are now part of our world, and will need to learn the laws and traditions of our kind."

I stood and made my way to dress for the celebration. His words resonated with me. I was a countess now. Even before he would change me, my whole life had changed drastically. And now I would have to learn about a whole world full of rules and laws that had nothing to do with the regular human world. I realized then that hunters existed in a world between two worlds: one world was that of humans who had no idea that vampires even existed; the other was the world of vampires, which was evidently more complex than we ever could have known.

But that was for tomorrow. I didn't want to think about that now. I focused instead on tonight. I could only imagine the looks on some of the faces tonight as the vampires in attendance realized that one who previously hunted them was now their countess. The final blow I could give as a hunter, I supposed. I smirked. My new life would be rather interesting, indeed.

I selected an emerald green strapless dress that showed off my curves a bit. As Gabriella came in to do my hair once again, I stole a quick glance in the mirror. It was still hard to believe that it was me staring back. Vito came in shortly after to lead me out to the second floor landing and present me to the local vampires.

I was actually astounded at how many there were. I had thought we were making a dent as we hunted vampires regularly, however the great room below was filled with them. It took everything in me to suppress the hunter instincts, and not search for the nearest weapon. However, the looks on some of the faces made my willpower stronger. Several faces showed recognition – those were vampires I had previous run-ins with.

The question now was whether or not my strong will would last. My surviving the night didn't depend on the vampires I was facing. Indeed, I knew now that it never had. Instead, my survival tonight depended entirely on me. I took a deep breath as Vito began leading me down the staircase, into my new life.

About the Author

Bethlyn has loved story telling in many forms since she was a child, and is proud to share this passion project with you all. She began writing Vampire Legacy back in high school with a friend as a game, lending a unique take on teenage banter in the story. Over the years, the story evolved and took on a life of its own, which you now hold in your hands.